FALCON SAGA

ROBERT WINTER

An Original Publication from Robert Winter Books

To request permission and all other inquiries, contact Robert Winter at robertwinterauthor@comcast.net or www.robertwinterauthor.com.

First Publication, January 2025

ISBN: 978-1-948883-18-4

Printed in the United States of America

For Peter,
who accompanies me on one adventure
after another and never lets me fall

MAP OF ICELAND

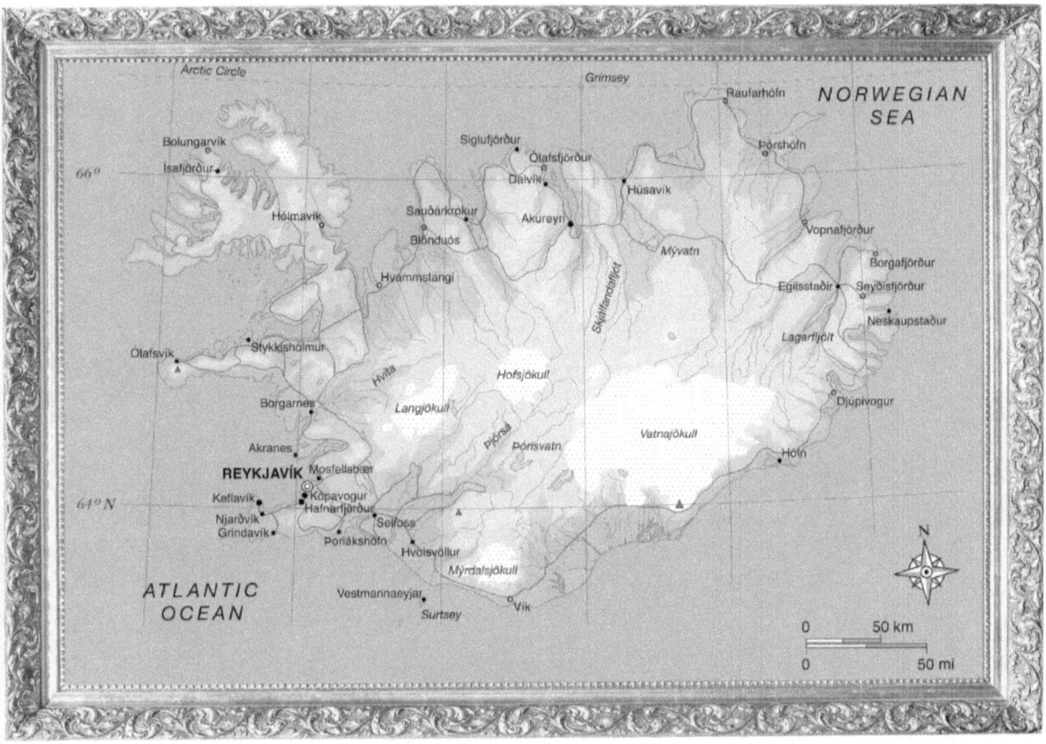

CONTENTS

CHAPTER

ONE

Magnús of the Hidden Ways wove light around himself to become invisible as he crouched on the limb of a rowan tree. The night was chilly, but only a faint breeze ruffled the leaves. Overhead, a tiny sliver of the waning moon shone like a sickle against the midnight-blue sky. The lights of an airplane bringing yet more tourists to Iceland distracted Magnús for a moment, but he couldn't afford to lose focus; human lives were at stake.

Brushing strands of his silver-blond hair back, he readied himself to attack a pair of large, dangerous creatures, all alone. Magnús cursed quietly. What were trolls doing this close to Reykjavik? And why had they dared to grab two hikers?

The fifteen-foot-tall beasts, lumpy and spiked as if made from lava, had their backs turned to Magnús's tree. They jostled and pushed at each other over some prize he couldn't quite glimpse. One punched the other in the arm with a noise like two boulders colliding, earning an angry bellow. The other swung back with what looked like a gnawed leg bone.

Scanning the carnage around the trolls, he spied torn jackets and other cold-weather clothing scattered on the ground. A bent and twisted backpack had been ripped open, its contents strewn across patches of snow that remained among the tree roots and scree. A splash of black across the front of the troll cave glistened wetly in the moonlight. It wasn't reflective and silvery like elf blood, so most likely it had come from a human.

That all signaled bad news for one or both of the missing English tourists. Was Magnús too late to do any good?

No, he could almost taste fear coming from the cave. At least one hiker was still alive, though in what condition he didn't know. Before the trolls could feast on their remaining captive, he had to act. He couldn't risk waiting for help, even if anyone had been near enough—and willing—to distract the monsters. As always, he would have to protect humans from supernatural threats by himself.

This is crazy. Magnús's stomach churned with adrenaline. Messing with one troll was difficult enough; two was a nightmare bordering on suicidal.

He wet his lips and reached into his pocket to retrieve a stone engraved with a rune, willing himself to become visible at the same time. "Týr One-hand, show favor to me in this battle," he whispered, a prayer to the war god. Týr had also risked Himself foolishly, as the gods chained the huge wolf Fenrir. Hopefully, Magnús wouldn't lose a hand as Týr had.

A sense of calm and strength grew in his body, starting with his head and seeping down through his limbs. He felt surer in his course as his invocation drew Týr's favor, stronger and faster. He would get the trolls out of the way, free whoever was still alive, and run. Yes.

Now.

Magnús hurled the stone with all his might as he sprang from the tree to the ground. It flared with blue light as it flew through the air, smack into the back of one troll's head. He crouched in sight of the trolls, ready to sprint up the side of the nearest hill where he'd laid a trap. He just needed them to take the bait.

The bait being Magnús.

The monster he'd hit raised a huge hand to feel its scalp for what hurt, grunting as it turned. It completely missed sight of Magnús's enchanted stone, still glimmering at its feet. The second troll was quick on the uptake, though, and rose on its stout legs. It lumbered toward Magnús, earth shaking beneath enormous feet as it picked up speed. The charging troll roared at him, its rank breath and spittle close enough to turn Magnús's stomach.

He dodged a wild swipe from a stony fist, rolling backward to land in a crouch that put him closer to his prepared battleground. He pulled a second stone from his pouch. At a whispered word, the rune on it burst into brilliant blue fire as he threw it straight at the nearest target. The missile hit the onrushing troll square in its left eye, making the creature rear back and howl in pain.

The other troll finally figured out what had hit him and stomped its way toward the fight. Magnús kept low but stayed in place until he was sure he had the attention of both creatures.

"That's right, you bastards. Chase me," he muttered.

One troll shot out a craggy hand to grab the trunk of a nearby birch. It ripped the tree from the ground in a torrent of dirt and leaves, then roared and shook the makeshift club. The tree-weapon slowed down that troll but made it all the more dangerous. The other had no finesse and simply charged toward Magnús.

He waited until they were twenty yards away, fifteen, ten... then darted away again, farther up the hillside. More of his dwindling supply of stones arced blue fire through the night over his shoulder. Loose stones slid under his left foot, and Magnús fell. The troll with the club bellowed and swung at him. The branches whistled as the weapon came down. Just in time, Magnús rolled out of the way. Fire burned on his back where the tree tore his sweater.

Magnús struggled to his feet and jumped away from a descending fist. He led the trolls on that way for a hundred yards, feeling blood drip down his back, fatigue burning his legs and in his lungs. Panting, he continued awkwardly up the hill sprinkled with the jagged volcanic rock that made up the setting he had prepared for a fight.

Spinning to send another missile, he drew the trolls on. The one with the uprooted tree swung it furiously and hit the other troll instead. But still they came at him, up the hill that rose higher and higher, blotting out the night sky, so tall it might be a mountain. A quick glance showed Magnús where he'd placed his trap minutes earlier, once he'd sized up the situation. He skidded to a halt right at the edge of it.

Turning, he pelted his two final runestones. The enraged trolls charged uphill at him with their boulder feet, an avalanche in reverse. The ground shook under their heavy tromping. Keeping an eye on that swinging birch, Magnús held his position as long as he dared.

The weaponless troll reached him first. It leaned down as it shambled forward, hands outstretched to grab Magnús. With its terrible strength, he couldn't afford to let it get hands on him. Yet he held his position, heart pounding. At the last possible second, he vanished, desperately *twisting* light to make himself invisible even as he whirled away and to the right.

The beast grasped at empty air as its momentum kept it staggering forward. It stepped past the barrier of Magnús's spell, shattering the magical illusion he'd created to hide that they actually battled at a jagged cliff's edge. Beyond that edge was nothing but night; below was a crevasse at least fifty yards deep. The troll hollered its fury and dismay as it stumbled over the cliff, plunging down into the darkness.

The second monster tried to skid to a halt when the illusion dissolved, but the birch club overbalanced it and kept it floundering. Hidden beside the troll, Magnús swung his leg in a round-house kick to its enormous backside. It skidded forward more on loose stones, then teetered at the edge of the cliff. Magnús exhaled in relief.

Too soon.

Some vestige of cunning seemed to tell the behemoth to use the birch tree to get its balance. It stretched a thick arm out, the weight of the tree helping it to regain footing. Before it could get both feet planted again, though, Magnús leapt forward and pushed against the troll with all his strength.

It was enough, barely. Uttering a bellow like rolling thunder, the troll pitched forward into space. Still clutching the birch, it fell after its fellow, cursing all the way down.

Panting, Magnús rested for a moment with his hands on his knees. The fall wouldn't be enough to kill the creatures, of course, unless they found themselves still trapped and exposed at sunrise. His mother Bryndís could have worked a spell to keep them frozen until the sun turned them to stone, but Magnús lacked that kind of power and polish. Before the trolls made their way back, he needed to see what aid he could give the humans.

Inside the cave, the horror that was a troll meal nearly made Magnús turn away and retch. The monsters had ripped apart one of the hikers, it looked like. The scent of violent death and troll inhabitation, more foul than untreated sewage, was enough to make him gag.

Moonlight picked up a silvery gleam that drew Magnús's attention. Something had been painted crudely on a rock face, reminiscent of a rune. He paused, curious, but then he noticed what lay above it on a ledge: a human head.

So, it was the man who died, Magnús thought, looking quickly away. Swallowing bile that burned his throat, he followed the trail of fear he could feel with his mind. It led him deeper into the cave. There he found a smallish pit, partly covered with a flat rock. The terror rising from the pit was like biting a piece of tin foil.

"I'm here to help," Magnús said in English.

Immediately a woman's voice cried out from inside the pit. "Please, please, get me out. Those things took Henry already. Please," the captive begged. Clarissa—he thought that was the name mentioned in the message that had alerted him.

"We have a few minutes. I tricked them out of the cave. Now, let me work."

Crouching at the edge of the pit, he contemplated the rock covering. Far too large for him to move alone, and if he pushed, it might tumble into the pit below, killing Clarissa. He would try asking the stone to help him, then. Magnús's reserve of magic was depleted from enchanting the stones and creating his illusion; he hoped he had enough left to get the captive free.

"Get as far back against the side of the pit as you can," Magnús called down. "Where you aren't under any part of the stone cover."

Laying hands on the rock, he let power fill him. Silently, reverently, he drew on the light of Álfheimur, the world made by the gods for the elves. It seeped into his body and out to the mortal world, burning his insides already because he'd overdone things somewhat. Yet he gritted his teeth and opened himself further to the magic.

A glow bloomed from within his hands, creating sharp shadows in the cavern. His bones became visible through his skin as the essence of Álfheimur filled them like a rising tide until it overflowed and spread throughout his limbs.

"What's that light?" Clarissa said. "What's happening?"

Magnús ignored her, focusing instead on the poetry of invocation. He knew he had it right when he could picture the spell in his head, its runes flickering like fire.

"Stone-friend, Rock-friend,
Solid as a mountain's root,
Show me how clever you are, good friend,
And lend me your aid under foot."

The rock remained firm to his touch, but the glow from his hands oozed across its surface. The covering rippled and softened like melting wax, then sagged in the center. Stone dripped lower and lower until it touched the bottom of the pit, forming rough steps in its surface. When the glow from Magnús's hands receded, the stairs again had the appearance and feel of rock, barely warm to the touch. Blessed coolness filled his limbs as he released his magic.

"Come up," he called out. "Quickly. It's safe."

Clarissa scrambled up the newly formed stairs and hurled herself at Magnús. "Thank you, thank you. Where's Henry? Can we get him out, too?"

Gently, Magnús disentangled himself. "I'm sorry. I was too late." Clarissa froze, shock visible in her eyes. "We need to be gone before the trolls come back."

Taking the trembling woman's arm, Magnús led her along the wall of the cavern and back to the opening. Her human eyes would be almost useless in the dark, so she shouldn't notice when they crept past the carnage that had been Henry. Magnús wasn't so lucky.

Why had the trolls done this wretched thing?

CHAPTER

TWO

INTERLUDE

Long, long ago, Óðinn the Allfather fashioned the first man and woman from two trees. With his brothers Vili and Vé, Óðinn bestowed life on them, and named them Askur and Embla.

Time passed, and Óðinn sent his ravens, Thought and Memory, ahead to tell Askur and Embla that he was coming to see them. Askur and Embla had managed to beget a surprising number of children, and they set about to prepare for the Allfather's visit. Embla tidied her children as best she could, but some of them had been out playing very late and were quite dirty.

Over a hill, a man wrapped in a gray cloak appeared, a raven on each shoulder. Embla knew Óðinn approached, and she was out of time to prepare. So, she hid the unkempt, playful children in a back room and bade them remain quiet.

The gray-cloaked wanderer arrived at their door and rapped on it sharply with his wooden staff. Askur, Embla, and the neatly scrubbed children all hurried outside to greet him and to enjoy a feast.

Looking over the assemblage, Óðinn asked Embla, "Are these all your children?" At this time, Óðinn still had both of his eyes, and they glinted at her like shards of obsidian.

Embla swallowed hard but said yes, these were all.

After the feast, Óðinn rose to leave. He bestowed a blessing on Askur, Embla, and their children, and started to turn away. Embla heaved a sigh of relief. Her little trick had not been discovered.

But then Óðinn turned back. The gray cloak shimmered away and revealed Allfather in his great and terrible majesty.

"You have tried to deceive me," he said to Askur and Embla in a voice of thunder. "Very well. From this day forward, the children you have hidden from me shall be hidden from all men."

After that, the wild, mischievous children could not be seen by men unless they wished it so. They ran away from Askur and Embla, who could not follow them or find them, and lived in the woods, the hills, and the moors. From those children came the race of huldufólk, sometimes also called elves. From the other children, all humans are descended.

CHAPTER

THREE

Altair shifted the bag of groceries awkwardly as he dug a key out of his front pocket. He rapped his knuckles twice on the door, then let himself in.

"Missus Carmichael? It's me," he called as he entered the small apartment and closed the door behind him.

The lady of the house rolled her wheelchair into the hall from her bedroom. She was in a pink bathrobe that matched the terrycloth turban covering her white hair.

"Oh, bless you, boy. I was just hankering for a glass of milk with my Oreos."

"Got you covered," Altair said with a wink, then carried the plastic shopping bag to her cramped kitchen to put away the groceries. He poured a glass of cold milk, calling out, "Get yourself in front of that TV and I'll bring you your snack."

Over the sound of rubber wheels on a hardwood floor, Altair heard Missus Carmichael give a small chuckle. "Too sweet for your own good, boy," she called out.

When he carried a tray with the milk and cookies into the

living room, he was greeted with a whistle and song from the birdcage in the corner.

"Hiya, Ladybird," he said.

The blue budgie did the same little dance she always put on when Altair visited, dipping her head as she whistled, fluttering from bar to bar in what looked like joy.

"That dang bird never acts so happy to see me," Missus Carmichael grumbled as she patted on a small table next to her wheelchair for the tray. She looked at the single milk glass and said, a little plaintively, "Aren't you gonna stay to watch the shows with me and Ladybird?"

"I wish I could," Altair said. "I've got to finish packing. We're leaving for the airport in about an hour."

Missus Carmichael sighed. "I don't know what business you got gallivanting off to another country."

Me neither, he thought.

Aloud, Altair said, "You know how it is. Everyone tells me this is the opportunity of a lifetime to shape my doctoral thesis."

"Shame for you to miss spring here, though," Missus Carmichael said. "Those baby ducks we been watching at the Common are about ready to cut loose."

"I know, I'm bummed, too," Altair said. "But, hey, I'll bring you a troll doll or something fun. You keep an eye on the ducks for me. Jason said he'll stop by in a few days to see if you need any more groceries, and I'll be back in two weeks."

Missus Carmichael muttered about Jason under her breath, but Altair heard her clearly. "Pretty but useless, that one."

"Aw, Jason's a good guy," Altair said. "He and Willa have been really great to me, letting me live with them and all while I'm in school."

"That Willa." Missus Carmichael shook her turbaned head. "She could curdle this here milk with that sour face of hers."

"Be nice," Altair begged. "She's just a little hard to get to know."

He didn't understand why Missus Carmichael had a problem with Jason and Willa. Jason was casual and breezy, not to mention hot. Willa was...okay, maybe not friendly, but super smart and serious and committed. They were a great balance for each other.

Living with them was such a relief, after all those years in the system. Then, it had seemed like every time he got close to someone, they'd be adopted or assigned to a different home. Or he'd make the mistake of relaxing into a situation, feeling like he might be able to stay there until he aged out, only to have the family replace him. Never an explanation, just—you're out, kid.

Missus Carmichael's snort brought Altair back from bad memories. "Iceland. Why can't you just finish your dissertation here?"

"Oh, I dunno." Altair fumbled with a loose thread on his sweater. "I've been having trouble settling on what power plant designs I want to pursue. My professor and Willa both think that seeing the geothermal technology they use in Iceland will help me focus and give me inspiration. That's why they pushed me to apply for the study grant."

"You think too much on what other people want from you," Missus Carmichael said. "What do *you* want?"

Not to be pushed out.

Not to start over again.

"I want to get my doctorate and build power plants," Altair said instead of the truth. He kissed Missus Carmichael on the cheek, whistled goodbye to Ladybird, and let himself out.

Two flights up, in his bedroom, he put a second sweater into the roll-aboard suitcase with gray duct tape patching it together in a few places. He looked around. Had he forgotten anything he might need in Iceland? Was there anything else to do before he left for the airport?

His narrow bed was made up, the small chest of drawers in the corner tidied, his stack of schoolbooks arranged neatly. *It's my space*, he thought fiercely, grateful that he didn't have to share any longer. In foster care, he'd always had to room with others, sometimes just one or two boys, sometimes with a dormitory full. What few belongings he could call his own in those days always went missing. Of course, his only possession of value now was his laptop, and that would go with him in his satchel to visit a land of snow and ice.

The thought made him shiver. Here he was, packing to ship off to the ass-end of nowhere, to a country where he knew no one, and where he couldn't speak the language. The flight to Iceland wouldn't be very long, but with the time change, he'd be far away from everything he knew. From every*one* he knew.

He'd been losing sleep over it, ever since he caved to the pressure and accepted the grant to go study there. Was this just a way for Willa and Professor Milton to get rid of him? The doubts ate at him, making him toss and turn far into the night.

When he did fall asleep, in his dreams, something was calling to him. That was maybe even more unnerving. Whatever it was, it whispered that he had a place in Iceland. That he was wanted. But that was just a bullshit dream. Other than his small quasi-family, no one had wanted him or welcomed him in a very long time.

"Why am I doing this again?" Altair asked out loud.

"Because it's just what you need for your dissertation. And if you don't finish soon..."

Willa stood in the doorway to his room, tall and thin, arms crossed over an MIT sweatshirt. Her black hair was pulled into a severe ponytail. With large, intense eyes devoid of makeup, she smiled tightly at him.

Altair grimaced. "I know, I know. That's what you and Professor Milton have been telling me for weeks."

Mixed with the message that if I don't get moving, you might need to find a more dedicated student for a roommate.

"Because it's true," Willa said. "You've been stuck for months now. The professor needs to make room for another teaching assistant, and Trausti is only going to help with your rent for so long. If you don't finish your doctorate soon, you'll be teaching science to junior high kids in South Boston instead of building power plants like you've dreamed."

She shrugged and added, "Your designs are solid but uninspired. You have the potential to be a great engineer, Altair. You're only going to find out how great if you get out of your rut here. The geothermal technologies in Iceland are innovative and exciting. You'll learn so much if you take full advantage of this opportunity."

Jason's shaggy blond hair and his grin full of white, straight teeth appeared behind Willa then as he leaned around the door. Resting one elbow on Willa's shoulder, tossing car keys in the other, he said, "Hi, bro. Ready to meet some sexy Vikings?"

Altair snorted. "Do you think anyone in Iceland will notice a short guy like me? Aren't the men all, like, six foot fifteen tall and blond? Besides, I don't speak any Icelandic."

"Way to stereotype," Willa said, adding an eye roll. "I've read that immigration is soaring in Iceland, so there should be all sorts of men. Plus, nearly the entire population speaks English. You probably ought to be careful anyway, about advertising you're queer."

Jason chuckled. "I think all those Nordic countries are really accepting. You'll be fine, kid. Go out there and grab some man meat." He nodded toward Altair's suitcase. "All packed?"

Altair sighed. "I think so, though I probably forgot something I'll need."

"You have the advance materials that Professor Sigmundsdóttir sent about the power plants you'll be touring together?" Willa asked.

"I do." Altair pointed to his black nylon satchel. "Printed and organized in a binder so I can study more on the plane." With another sigh, he looked around his room once more. "You aren't going to sublet this while I'm gone, are you?"

Willa snorted. "You're in Iceland for two weeks, not two years. Stop worrying. You'll be fine if you just finish your doctorate."

"We should get going to the airport," Jason said. "Rush hour traffic to Logan will be a bitch."

As Altair gathered his suitcase and satchel to follow his roommates down the hallway, the buzzer rang. Willa pressed the intercom button, and Uncle Trausti's voice came through. She buzzed the street door open, then turned to look Altair up and down.

"Don't be so nervous," she said. "It's an easy flight, you'll be in Reykjavik by dawn, and you'll have a day to prepare before you get started with the university tour."

Jason nudged Altair's shoulder. "I hear there's a museum devoted to dicks. You definitely should go sightseeing first and check it out."

Altair chuckled nervously. "You're kidding, right?"

Jason flashed his big smile again. "Only way to know is if you go look for it."

Willa grimaced at Jason and grumbled, "He doesn't have time to sightsee."

Trausti swept into the apartment then, tall and commanding. Dark blond hair gleamed, and his dark suit looked expensive and out of place in what was essentially a university student apartment. Altair tucked his hands into pockets rather than reaching for the hug he knew would not come from his uncle.

"Altair, my boy. I'm so excited for you to take this journey. Back to the land of our ancestors, yes?"

"I still can't believe my grandmother came from Iceland," Altair murmured, a bit resentful of his uncle's Nordic height. "I don't look anything like the pictures I've seen of people there."

"That's your mother's blood showing through." Trausti tousled Altair's short hair, then stepped back. "I didn't know her, of course, but her people are usually dark."

"Her people?"

"She was Arabic, wasn't she?"

"Well, her parents were," Altair agreed. "Mom was born in the States."

Trausti dismissed that with a wave of his hand. "As I said. I'm surprised your father was drawn to her. Perhaps it was the exotic features. Though, of course, Fálki left her, too. He simply lost interest at some point, I expect."

Altair choked back the instinct to defend his mother. After all, it wasn't Trausti's fault that his brother Fálki had abandoned his wife and child.

Resentment suddenly flared bright in Altair. He pictured his father as he'd last seen him, when he was three years old. Or maybe he was remembering photos: His dad in his uniform as a pilot for a regional airline, short like Altair ended up, but with blond hair instead of the reddish-brown Altair had from his mother.

Altair remembered being carried in his mom's arms that awful day, as they waved goodbye from a fence next to the airfield. Dad climbed into the cockpit, started the engine, and taxied away. That was the last time they saw him.

If Altair had known his father was leaving them and had no plans to return, would he have hugged him harder? Would Dad have stayed if Altair had been more interesting and less awkward? Would Altair have avoided the foster system after Mom died?

Trausti clapped his hands suddenly, the sound making Altair jump. He must have been standing there, wool-gathering, for quite a while.

"I'm sorry," Altair said. "I think I dozed off or something."

"Don't sweat it, bro," Jason said easily. "You've been stressing about this trip. It's sure to have messed up your sleep. You ready to head out now?"

"One last thing before you go," Trausti said.

He reached into the breast pocket of his suit and brought out a small, hard-bound book. It seemed to have a red cover...no, it was more beige, and sort of mottled.

Altair blinked again, and the book had a pink cover, with a floral design. He shook his head. He must really be exhausted, the way his eyes were playing tricks on him.

Trausti held out the book reverently. "This was my mother's diary," he said. "She wrote about growing up in Iceland, and then about her experiences when she emigrated to the United States. I'd like you to have this, my boy. It will keep you company when you feel isolated in Iceland and remind you that you are connected to the land."

Altair reached for the book, but Trausti jerked it back. He leaned closer, dark eyes burning into Altair's. "This is very precious to me. You understand that, don't you?"

"Y-yes, sir."

"And you will keep it safe, won't you?"

"Yes. Very safe." His own voice seemed to come from a distance. All he could see were Trausti's eyes, like obsidian.

"Best to keep it private. In fact, don't think about it too much. Just take comfort in knowing you have a tangible connection to your homeland."

Altair took the book in both of his hands, holding it gently, by the edges. A shudder passed through him at the touch. Opening his satchel, he tucked the book into one of its interior pockets, made sure it was secure, and buckled the bag's clasp again.

The room swam for a moment, and Altair reached out a steadying hand. Willa took it.

"You're fine, Altair," she said bracingly. "Just low blood sugar. You didn't eat enough lunch."

"Right," he said, a bit dazed. "I didn't eat enough lunch. Um, sorry. What were we talking about?"

Jason chuckled. "About getting your ass to the airport in time to catch this flight. It's going to change your life, man. Just watch!"

CHAPTER

FOUR

Magnús watched from twenty yards away as the hiker Clarissa huddled in the care of the Search and Rescue team; a paramedic was treating her for shock. His friend Karl stood by his side, bundled in his SAR jacket, chewing his lip thoughtfully as he scratched his red beard.

"Do you think that other trolls might similarly be getting aggressive?" Karl asked, his voice tight.

Magnús glanced around at the other humans nearby before he answered. Everyone in earshot seemed to be an SAR member and therefore Icelandic. That meant they probably had a passing knowledge of the supernatural races with which they shared the country, even if they wouldn't admit outright to believing. Karl had more experience than most humans with the huldufólk and some of the other inhabitants, what with his own father being a witch. SAR team members who worked with Karl might be "in" on the danger of trolls or might not.

"Hard to say, but I wouldn't rule it out," Magnús answered quietly, to be safe. "Are your bosses going to be able to keep this attack out of the press?"

"They'll have to, won't they? Everyone at the top is schooled hard on keeping our secrets."

Magnús nodded. *No being not of Iceland shall be told of or allowed to spread knowledge of Iceland's super-nature.* In the millennium since the Alþingi of Realms agreed to the First Covenant, violations were traditionally dealt with by the race of the offending party, but the other races could—and at times had been forced to—intervene to honor it.

"Even apart from the Covenant, imagine what would happen if word spread we have elves and trolls and witches around." Karl shuddered. "Forget the volcano sightseers. We'd be swarmed with people looking for sightings, or foreign tourists hunting for a new kind of trophy."

"As if a gun would stop a troll from ripping apart a human," Magnús said. "If you're going to keep this murder quiet, though, you need a cover story. Do you have one ready?"

"Not yet." Karl sighed, then shook his head as he kept eyes on his crew. He tugged his russet beard in frustration. "Almost makes me wish Iceland had some wolves or bears we could blame. Selling the story to international media that an arctic fox decapitated and dismembered the hiker...oof."

"Will you be able to handle Clarissa's memories?"

"Pabbi will."

Karl's father was not the most gifted witch, but skillful enough to work memory charms. "This case will be tricky, making her forget trolls and me but knowing that her boyfriend is dead."

"We'll work out a story first before Pabbi visits her dream for the spell." Karl pulled from a pocket of his heavy jacket the tool Magnús had enchanted for Karl to contact him. "Speaking of spells, we were lucky you were near enough to help when this reached you. At least we got one of the hikers out alive."

Magnús took the silver mirror in a rounded frame of ash wood and examined the runes he'd carved onto the glass, making sure its spell held. As he worked, he murmured, "Those trolls were brazen, snatching two humans so close to Reykjavik. I haven't heard of an event like this in, oh, decades perhaps. Someone will hold them to account for breaking the Covenant. If not the Mountain King, then others."

Karl grimaced, his squarish face worried. "I hope so, but you're more optimistic than me. We've had an uptick in disappearances in the last month or so. I'm starting to wonder if they were all troll attacks."

Magnús grunted. Tourists often got in trouble hiking the glaciers because they didn't come prepared. An American family even drove their van onto the ice, oh, maybe one or two winters back. This year, though, an actively erupting volcano was bringing in a lot more tourists than normal, with visitors taking huge risks to see lava flow up close.

"Do you mean disappearances just around here, or is it more widespread than that?" he asked.

"We usually have one or two incidents a year where a tourist can't be found, probably because they fell into a crevasse or a waterfall and the body wasn't discovered. But a higher number than usual this year have vanished with no trace, all over Iceland. With what you discovered today, it could all be troll related." Karl shook his head. "If this continues, it will be hard to keep quiet. I don't see the trolls policing themselves, so others will have to act."

Magnús frowned. That sounded ominous, echoing of the battles of eight or nine centuries past that had led to destruction and death throughout Iceland. Surely it wouldn't come to that again. The Mountain King would keep the peace and bring his trolls back in line. Eventually.

But in the meantime, tourists were missing, maybe at the hands of other trolls. If so, it was likely they'd already suffered the fate of Henry. If Magnús got going right away, though, perhaps he could find survivors still. Or figure out why some trolls were making such a brazen move.

Magnús sighed to himself; he hadn't visited home or spent time with friends in months, because there always seemed to be some threat to investigate or attack to rebuff. Until other elves realized Magnús was correct about danger to their civilization, though, he would simply have to keep moving forward.

"I'm inclined to agree with you. If there's one tangle of trolls getting out of hand, there could be more. Can you get me a list of locations where the missing people were last seen? I'll start there."

Karl frowned at him. "We can handle it."

"Too dangerous," Magnús said, shaking his head. "Even a whole team of SAR wouldn't be able to drive a troll off."

"Always this," Karl replied with a huff. "It isn't your job to keep every human in Iceland safe from the supernatural—"

Magnús raised a hand to signal Karl to wait because he felt a tickle in his mind, near his left ear. The echo of a tolling bell, a scent of ocean breeze after a storm had passed—it was the essence of his cousin Ólafur's mental voice, but with that tinny quality one got from evoking a sigil. Óli must be far away, perhaps at his family's farmhouse in Hamarinn, if he needed a sigil's help to bridge the miles between their minds. Still, the voice in Magnús's head was as clear as if Ólafur stood next to him.

«Magnús of the Hidden Ways, it's urgent. I have terrible news from the witch Diwata Pétursdóttir—»

«One moment, Óli,» Magnús responded. "I'll find you later," he said aloud to Karl and clapped him on the shoulder.

"We aren't finished with this discussion," Karl called as Magnús walked away.

Away from the humans and their noise, he made himself invisible again and sank down, back against a tree. Drained though he was, he fortunately didn't have to draw on the light of Álfheimur to use his invisibility and mind-speech, as those were gifts to the huldufólk from Óðinn Allfather.

Awareness flickered in that spot near his left ear. Magnús composed himself and let his awareness grow, signaling his readiness to talk.

«Magnús, finally, you spare me a moment.» Ólafur's voice carried an edge of strain that was unusual in the laid-back elf Magnús had known all his four hundred years.

Magnús snorted. «Just tell me what you want.»

«You remember my friend, Diwata Pétursdóttir? The pretty baker? She's the witch with the cottage by the river—»

«I remember her breads are fantastic. Wait, you're spending time with a human? Watch out or Lars will lay into you.»

«Leave my brother out of this, would you? Listen, Diwata is here in Hamarinn. She rushed over to ask me to reach you. She has just received a terribly prophecy—a horrific invasion of Iceland by forces of evil sorcery. You are needed to save us.»

"An invasion? But that's impossible," Magnús scoffed aloud, then said mentally, «No sorcerer has ever been able to invade Iceland.»

«I know that, Cousin,» Ólafur interrupted, sounding exasperated at the obvious. «Every one of us honors the Landvættir who protect the land from supernatural invasion. Don't forget I was with you in the vanguard when that madman Hitler attempted to invade Iceland for magical artifacts.»

«Ah, that was exciting,» Magnús returned. «Remember when Bergrisi the Giant helped us tear through the army Hitler secretly sent along to protect his Nazi sorcerers?»

«That's more your world than mine,» Ólafur said with a mental shudder. Magnús understood; his cousin was a farmer, not a fighter. «Nevertheless, Diwata says a magical invasion is coming very soon, and the Nornir named Magnús of the Hidden Ways to stand against it.»

«That's surprisingly specific; prophecies are usually more vague. But why bring this to you, Óli?»

Magnús caught a mental blush from his cousin.

«Diwata and I like to play video games and talk about the metal scene in Reykjavik sometimes, so she knew right where to find me. We have plans to go see this awesome band, you should come—»

«Great, but why am I involved in this prophecy at all?»

«I don't know why you're mentioned, but I think we should meet. You, me, and Diwata.»

«Bryndís as well,» Magnús added. «If this is a true scrying, we will need her guidance.»

«Of course it's a true scrying.» Ólafur's mental voice sounded indignant. «Diwata is a very good witch. Her gift to see the future is amazing. Remember last year, when she predicted an earthquake would cause that bridge to collapse, and you were able to warn the human authorities through your friend Karl? And when she saw that trouble was brewing between the dwarves and the dark elves, so Lady Bryndís was able to mediate before things got out of hand?»

«All right, all right. I meant no disrespect to your friend. I'll come to Hamarinn as quickly as I can, if you'll bring Diwata to Bryndís's hall.»

If Magnús had the strength, he'd open the Hidden Ways to get to Hamarinn directly. As it was, he'd drained himself with battling the trolls and bespelling the rock that kept Clarissa penned. He hurried after Karl to beg a lift back toward Reykjavik.

CHAPTER
FIVE

Bryndís stood watch on a promontory next to the giant, Bergrisi. Both elf and land wight had eyes fixed on the ocean, and on the ship advancing toward the coast. Its prow was carved elaborately, and its large, spread sail valiantly captured the wind.

Bending low to be heard, Bergrisi rumbled, "The humans are coming back."

Bryndís considered the ship. "More arrive this time. I wonder what they intend?"

These weren't the first humans to reach their land, of course. A few thin, starved, and ragged men who called themselves monks had come, years earlier, from a place called Ireland. Bryndís and some others of the hidden folk had taken pity on the wretches and helped them build shelters and find food. Those monks had treated the huldufólk as angels sent by the singular god they believed it.

That had puzzled the huldufólk, of course, because even now

the Æsir were frequent visitors to the land. Óðinn Allfather, Þór the Thunderer, trickster Loki, and the rest were not only honored from afar but welcomed to hearth and feast at every opportunity.

Yet the monks seemed to know nothing of the Æsir. They would hear no argument that the huldufólk had nothing to do with that Christ person they called upon so frequently. But peculiar beliefs aside, the Irish monks made little trouble.

In later years, some of the huldufólk had reported isolated encounters with a different type of human, one or two at a time. Unlike the darker, ascetic monks, these blond and warlike humans had generally taken one look at the stark beauty and natural wonders of the land...and turned away. Its snows were too harsh, its game animals too small, its forests, falls, and geysers filled with spirits and other things that unnerved the warriors.

And yet, here was a larger contingent, apparently of the same origin as the warriors. Bryndís with her keen eyes could see blond hair, swords, thick coats, and leggings that would be useful protection in a battle. Were they coming to make war on the huldufólk?

Hearing her silent question, Bergrisi the Giant rumbled, "I don't think so. At least, they have no magic. I'm sure of that. Would humans dare make trouble here without a sorcerer or witch?"

Bryndís patted his tree-like arm. "With you and the other Landvættir standing watch on the coast, we need not fear a magical invasion. Allfather himself has said so."

Bergrisi preened, his pleased grin an amusing sight on a face the size of a boulder.

"We must wait and see," Bryndís concluded.

Before long, the ship ground ashore on the beach below where Bryndís and Bergrisi stood, unseen unless they willed otherwise. Twenty or so men, and more than a few women, climbed out of the ship. As they prepared for camp, their voices carried on the wind. A tall, thickly built man, clean shaven, wearing a fine cloak and conical helmet, seemed to be in charge. He gestured and bellowed his orders. A woman dressed in a similarly fine cloak also seemed important, as several of the women and some of the men took her direction.

Bryndís closed her eyes, reaching to hear the thoughts behind the language that was foreign to her. It had worked with the monks, and it seemed it would work with these people as well.

"Ingólfur Arnarson, he calls himself," Bryndís told Bergrisi, gesturing at the one in charge. "These are his wife and his household, come from a place they call Norway. Their name for our country is Iceland. They intend to settle here, I believe."

Among the wights and other creatures, the humans already there were regarded variously as amusing or as food. Doubtless, some of her people would not welcome the newcomers.

"I will whistle for Veðurfölnir," Bergrisi said, musing. "He will bear the news to the others."

At that moment, the ground began to groan and shift slightly. It was but one of the frequent tremors that signified the life force of their country, but the humans on shore called out to each other in alarm. The quake was in keeping with the recent increase in volcanic eruptions and tremors the country had experienced.

Are these eruptions and quaking omens? Bryndís wondered.

Although the tremor subsided in moments, the men and women continued their consternation for some time. Their assimilation would not be easy until they learned to accept the dynamic nature of this land of fire and ice.

A hostile welcome from the land and its inhabitants to a warlike people who were already uneasy in their new home.

Well, this could be interesting, she thought.

CHAPTER

SIX

An hour after catching up with Karl's SAR crew and persuading them to detour south of Reykjavik, Magnús walked quickly through the town of Hafnarfjörður. His path led into a rock-strewn meadow, verdant with grasses and yellow and purple wildflowers sprung from the rich soil.

The early-blooming lupines were a minor irritant to Magnús, since the plant was not native to Iceland and had proved invasive. Not that it caused harm, and in truth its flowers were quite beautiful. Still, lupine was one more proof that the land wights that guarded Iceland from outside threats were not the absolute protection some of the huldufólk claimed.

He paused at a clearing to admire the harbor below, where boats of various sizes ranging from working vessels to pleasure crafts floated in glittering water. Turning away, he climbed down a winding path to reach a rocky outcropping nearly concealed by small trees: the entrance to Hamarinn. The stone face of the cliff at that place was four or five yards tall and craggy.

Enough time had passed during the drive that Magnús could again access some of his magic. He wove light around the rock wall to illuminate the entrance no human could find. Glyphs on an interior-facing crevice responded to his presence, glowing to reveal the doorway into the elf-town. He pressed against it, and the stone face swung inward to allow Magnús to enter.

The way before him twisted down, into the rocky depths of Iceland. The soft, blue glow of lightstones set into the wall and floor of the passage guided Magnús, flaring ahead as they reacted to his elf-blood, fading behind as he walked on.

Soon enough, he took the last turning and stepped out of the passage onto a ledge overlooking the huldufólk village. When he was young, he'd asked if the elf-town Hamarinn was actually in Miðgarður, or if it somehow existed in a borderland of Álfheimur, realm of the light elves. No one he'd met could say for sure.

The subterranean settlement lay in the middle of a grassy vale, under a cavern roof glistening with embedded stones. Instead of a static glow, the enchanted stones that lined the cavern ceiling formed a rippling and flowing mosaic that scattered patches of light and shadow on the valley below, much as if clouds scudded across the face of the sun.

As was only right, Magnús paused and silently thanked Freyja, goddess of magic, for her teachings to the huldufólk. The spell-craft required to create even one sunstone, which held its light for centuries, never failed to humble him. Each stone was a piece of nearly indestructible glass that had once been a shard of glacial ice, the sunlight that had flowed through it captured by magic. Tens of thousands of sunstones painted the roof cavern with blue and gold, even during the long dark of winter.

Magnús made his way down to the valley floor, which was dotted with farms, outbuildings, and several homes. Scents of hay and manure drifted to him from the pens of sheep and cattle. Freshly turned earth and ripening vegetables teased his nose, along with wildflowers and the smell of clear water from a briskly running stream.

The light cast over the fields by the enchanted cavern ceiling was softer than that of the world above. Ólafur had tried to explain why it was sufficient for growing crops; Magnús hadn't listened. Agriculture was not among his interests, though it fascinated his cousin.

Along a path sat the large hall where he had grown up. The chieftain's longhouse that was the central building of Hamarinn stretched more than fifty yards long, befitting his mother Bryndís's status as gyðja of the elf-town.

"Practical," Bryndís had called the design in one of her lectures to Magnús on his legacy. "Long ago, the Vikings and settlers arrived from Norway and constructed their longhouses. We watched how the Norsemen erected their building, with its rows of high posts to support the roof and walls of turf and sod. We liked the way humans gathered for warmth and comfort, how they kept their animals safe through long winters. We liked the hearth fires within, the storage and crafting areas, even the methods for dealing with their refuse and waste. And so we adopted the longhouse."

Those early turf structures had been covered in wattle and daub and floored with pounded earth. Over the centuries, huldufólk craftspeople had transformed their version of the structure into something solid but graceful. The earthen walls of the Hamarinn longhouse were covered in sheets of finely beaten metal, carved with runes of health and happiness. Its window frames were painted in bright and varied colors. The thatched roof remained but was these days covered in flowers.

Even some lupine, Magnús noticed with a snort.

"Ah, the traitor pays a visit," a voice sneered from behind Magnús, drawing him to an abrupt stop. "Killed any more of our native creatures? Are you here to find victims to persecute in your humans-first campaign?"

Magnús's jaw tightened as he turned to face the speaker. "Lars

Berkisson. You must be desperate if you're grubbing for supporters here."

Lars gave Magnús a tight smile, his steel-gray eyes narrowing. "I came to offer comfort to Vörður, and to tend to his affairs while he rots in the cell where you put him. Tell me, Magnús. How many more of your own people will you try to destroy in your self-hatred?"

"Vörður put himself in that cell when he stole a human baby and tried to pass himself off as the infant. He ignored the edict laid down by Queen Hildur, risked violating the First Covenant, and in any event, the act was despicable. Changelings have been forbidden for decades."

Lars laughed. "Of course, you and Bryndís are too modern to gather servants in the old ways. But we who honor the ancient customs have long known that if we must tolerate non-magical humans on our shores, then they are best taken as babes. Those raised from infancy make for superior attendants and retainers. The queen has been led astray by your misplaced devotion to mortals, but I have confidence she'll return to tradition."

Magnús clenched his jaw, determined to keep his temper. "A tradition of bigotry and false piety, pretending the gods want us to use humans as pets or chattel."

"Well, isn't that what Sigurjón was to you? A pet?"

The twist to Lars's upper lip enraged Magnús. Although Lars had been back from his exile for nearly a fifth of a century, Magnús's every encounter with him brought them close to battle. With a tremendous effort of will, Magnús refrained from pulling the dagger tucked in his belt.

"Sigurjón was as much a child of the gods as you once were, Lars," he said through gritted teeth. "The path you follow leads to Hel's sunless lands, though you lie to your followers and promise them Valhöll."

Lars shook his head in a way that infuriated Magnús.

"Álfheimur is the true home of our people. Those who hear my words long only for a return to the days before men invaded our shores. Before they killed our trees, stole our magic, and built their abominable cities."

"The gods led mortals here to Iceland, *Cousin*. Your brand of fanaticism sets those who believe you against the will of the Æsir. And I, for one, look forward to a reckoning."

With that, Magnús strode away. He didn't trust himself to spend one more minute in the presence of the vile creature who had murdered his beloved Sigurjón.

CHAPTER

SEVEN

Still seething from his encounter with Lars, Magnús called ahead to the longhouse to announce his presence. «Bryndís, my mother. May I meet with you?»

The door opened soundlessly as he approached though no servant was to be seen; Bryndís's magic, no doubt. She emerged from a back room to meet him in the main hall. As tall as Magnús, her honey-golden hair hung in a braid over her shoulder and down a loose-flowing green dress. It was embroidered with silver, in a style that had been popular a century earlier. Her sapphire-blue eyes and a smooth face that belied her centuries shone from within as she briefly touched Magnús on the shoulder.

"My son, welcome home. I have not seen you since that unfortunate business with Vörður. Are you well?"

"I am, my mother," Magnús replied, matching her formality. He loved Bryndís fiercely but sometimes he wished she could be a little less cold, a little more comforting. His mother was the undisputed leader of Hamarinn, powerful in magic, well-respected, and a close advisor to Queen Hildur. But warm? Forthcoming? No, Magnús could not use those words for his mother.

She leaned back slightly, eyes intent on his. Somewhat reproachfully, she said, "I could feel your anger at Lars Brother's-son as you drew near. After all this time, can you find no forgiveness in your heart?"

Magnús grunted but otherwise refused to respond.

Bryndís sighed, then gestured for him to follow her. "Come. Ólafur and the young human are here already."

She led him into one of the more formal chambers, where Ólafur and Diwata were seated at an oval oak table. Magnús pulled out a heavy, carved chair for himself, across from his cousin. Bryndís seated herself at the head in the largest chair—almost a throne. She sat straight-backed, light catching her golden hair and flaring like a crown.

Diwata lounged sideways across her chair, denim-clad legs dangling. Olive skin, with dark, wavy hair and small eyes that looked almost black. She was toying with a silver charm on her necklace. It dangled over a white tee-shirt, which bore the name of an old punk band Ólafur used to go on about. A small basket in front of her was covered in a white cloth, and the mouthwatering smell of freshly baked bread rose from it.

Ólafur sat right beside Diwata. His simple tan trousers and green shirt looked slightly work-worn from his time in the fields. Since the last time Magnús met him, his reddish-gold hair had been shaved on both sides, and the rest was pulled into a bun; Magnús thought he looked ridiculous.

A plate before Ólafur contained a half-eaten piece of a very dark bread, slathered with butter. Magnús said hopefully, "Is that rugbraud?"

Diwata grinned at him. "Yep. Pulled it out just before I came. Want some?" When he nodded eagerly, she peeled away the cloth to cut him a slice, slid it onto a plate, and pushed it in his direction.

"Gods, that's good," Magnús said, rolling his eyes happily at the taste of delicious bread. "Óli is right, you are an accomplished baker, and it is a pleasure to meet you again. But please explain about this prophecy of invasion, which we all know is impossible."

Ólafur bristled, but Diwata just snorted at Magnús. "The Nornir sent me a vision as sharp and clear as I've ever received. You want to ignore that? Fine. The invasion will be on your stubborn head."

Bryndís spoke calmly. "No one doubts your word, Diwata Pétursdóttir. Will you share the memory? One of us might notice a detail that would otherwise be overlooked."

Diwata grimaced. "Yeah, I figured you'd ask. I have no objection." She pulled the chain of her silver necklace over her head, then tucked it carefully into a pocket of her jeans.

Magnús suddenly realized that he had been unable to sense Diwata's mind until she took off the charm. He narrowed his eyes. That was pretty powerful magic, to keep out the huldufólk's natural ability to read thoughts and emotions. He wondered why she had it and where it came from.

Then he looked sideways at Ólafur. His cousin had mentioned spending time with Diwata and had been a bit cagey about it, even embarrassed...

"Thank you, child," Bryndís said. "My brother's son Ólafur, would you make the connection with Diwata? I will create communion among us so we all may experience the memory."

"Of course, Lady Bryndís," Ólafur answered. He turned in his chair to meet Diwata's gaze. "Relax and breathe, like you're composing yourself for sleep."

She nodded and gave him a small smile. "I trust you."

The usual subtle glow appeared behind Ólafur's cornflower-blue eyes as he called upon the power of Álfheimur to guide him into Diwata's memories. Magnús experienced a small pang of jealousy; Ólafur found it so easy to reach a human mind, something Magnús himself had great difficulty with.

His own facility with the Hidden Ways was useful, though, albeit imperfect. Perhaps in another hundred years he'd be able to use his gift without it draining his magic and leaving him useless for a time.

When Ólafur nodded in Bryndís's direction, his mother drew on Álfheimur's magic as well. The glow that danced around her head grew in intensity as she invoked the god of wisdom.

"Cunning Mímir, we children, beloved of the Æsir, seek counsel and secret knowledge. It is I, Bryndís Meadbearer who asks, who quenched your thirst when your head was severed from its body."

The spell seemed to find favor with Mímir, because the glimmer around Bryndís's head extended to Ólafur, and then to Magnús and Diwata. Double vision blurred the table in the great hall as Magnús shared in watching the memory unfurl.

DIWATA SAT ON THE GROUND, in jeans and a loose tee-shirt, a leather-bound book open on her lap. An apple seed, a ripe apple, and a wrinkled, dried one lay in a line before her. Dark hair hung about her face as she peered down into a stone bowl full of water.

The water shimmered and took on a silvery sheen. Across the surface, an image of fire and flood appeared. Enormous trolls hurled boulders at elves on horseback, who were trying to bring them down. Humans bearing rifles and assault weapons clambered up a beach, supporting the trolls. Hags wearing torn and stained robes hurled orbs of fire at the defending elves. Other creatures Diwata had no name for—some beautiful, some hideous—crawled from the waters or emerged from fissures in the earth.

Behind the melee, on a hill or cliff, a tall figure in black surveyed the battle. They seemed to be a man, from their wide shoulders and stance. His face was hidden by a broad hat brim. When he raised his hands, lightning fell from the sky, striking down elves as well as other nonhuman creatures apparently standing with them.

Behind the man on the hill arose a figure five times his size, wreathed in flame, horns sprouting from its forehead. It seemed to Diwata a chain bound the monster to the man in the hat, now silhouetted by the creature's fiery form. The man pointed, and the monster belched forth a blue blaze that killed dozens of defenders.

The carnage in her vision made Diwata want to weep. A voice resonated in her ears then, as hollow and old as wind whistling down a sunless cavern:

"—*The Falcon's swift flight on metal wings will be hidden from the Bull. Under the new moon, it will deliver the Bishop's Shackles into the hands of the Black Priest, who will pave the way for terrible armies to vanquish the defenders of Iceland. For good or ill, Magnús of the Hidden Ways must stand against the forces drawn by the Black Priest, or all is lost.—*"

The memory faded, but Magnús realized his heart was pounding. The destruction in that vision was awful. And the human army—how could such a thing happen? What did any of it have to do with him, that he would be named so precisely?

Across the table, Bryndís's speculative eyes met his. "The new moon is but three days away," she observed. "The Nornir have pulled the thread tight, my son. You are named in the prophecy, so this must be your path."

Magnús ground his teeth. "I can't abandon everything to search for a falcon and a priest. There are hundreds of gyrfalcons in the Northeast. Thousands. Am I supposed to go hunting for a single falcon in the mountains there?" He snorted explosively; his chair creaked as he leaned forward. "Trolls are snatching humans, coming closer to the cities even. Some of the victims may still be alive."

Ólafur leaned closer as well, folding his hands before him. "Cousin, I know your love of humans. But surely you see this threat is against our kind and humans as well. Others can look into this troll business."

"Who?" Magnús shot back. "Who but me and maybe two or three others cares enough about humans to protect them from trolls and ghosts, and even the worst of the huldufólk?"

"Leave Lars out of it," Ólafur responded with heat. "I know your history with my brother. But this is far larger than one or two lost humans."

"Ooh, brutal," Diwata murmured. Both elves looked at her, blinking at the interruption. Before their argument could resume, she twisted around in her chair and asked Bryndís, "Do you have any idea what the Nornir meant, about a falcon and a black priest and shackles?"

Bryndís steepled her elegant fingers, light glinting from her rings, considering. "The terms whisper to me, but no, I do not know what they mean. In ages past, many of the humans who devoted themselves to witchcraft were also priests of the Christian gods. But other Christians sometimes attacked or even burned them alive." She shook her head. "In truth, I never fully understood."

Diwata sighed. "It was a terrible time. Anyway, the last witchcraft trials were in the sixteen hundreds. After that, we witches learned to hide better. But I've never heard of any modern witches still affiliated with Christianity."

Her eyes turned down to the wooden surface of the table as she shuddered and said more quietly, "That...*creature* that breathed fire was terrifying. Was it a fire giant, do you suppose, called out of Muspellsheimur?"

Bryndís said, "It was far larger than any fire giant I have ever encountered and seemed more powerful."

"Why would a falcon be flying on metal wings?" Ólafur asked as he reached for more bread.

Diwata slapped his hand away but cut him another slice.

"Maybe it's one of those drone things tourists like to use. Perhaps a brand name."

Bryndís shook her head slowly. "The threat is of an invasion, and this falcon is key. Thus, it seems unlikely the Nornir are speaking of one of our own gyrfalcons or of a toy."

"Fair enough." Diwata covered the remaining bread and set aside her knife, then crossed her arms and shifted in her chair. "I think there are falcons all over the world, though. Talk about a needle in a haystack."

"The prophecy mentioned the Bull as well," Ólafur said. "Do you suppose it could mean Griðungur?"

A tutor's recitation from long ago played in Magnús's head: *The mighty Griðungur, in form a gigantic bull, one of the four Landvættir that protect Iceland from sorcerous invasion...* No other bull that might be relevant came to mind. "Let's assume so. Griðungur protects the western shore of Iceland. So, does that suggest this falcon is arriving from the west?"

Ólafur tilted his chair back on its legs. "Greenland is the nearest country to the west of us, but it's unlikely a bird could make that journey on its own. Perhaps the falcon is being carried to our shores?"

Bryndís made a small gesture with her fingers, and Ólafur's chair abruptly landed on all four legs again, leaving him with a startled look in his eyes. She said, "A falcon could be blown from Greenland on a storm, perhaps, though the weather has been fair for several days. A ship? The falcon could be a pet, caged and carried aboard a vessel bound for Iceland."

Diwata sat upright, almost jumping from her own chair in excitement. "Could 'metal wings' refer to an airplane?"

"Ah, very clever," Ólafur said, smiling at her. "An airplane arriving from the west, bringing this Falcon and something called the Bishop's Shackles. That would fit."

"But is it a literal falcon?" Magnús asked. "Diwata, is it

possible for you to scry again? Perhaps the Nornir will reveal more about such a dangerous threat."

Diwata hesitated, then gave a sharp, nervous nod.

Bryndís's chair scraped the stone floor as she rose gracefully and extended a hand to the witch. "Come, join me. There is another room more suitable, and I will help." Her lips curved in a rare smile. "Skuld owes me a small favor."

Magnús gaped at Bryndís. "One of the Nornir owes you a favor?"

"My son, many things have happened in my life of which you have no knowledge."

Ólafur met Magnús's gaze and rolled his eyes slightly; Magnús returned a rueful look. It was just like when they were young, a few centuries back. Bryndís had always been slightly disapproving of the newer huldufólk who lacked her gravity.

The cousins followed Bryndís and Diwata through a small doorway, down a hall lined in wood paneling and graced with fixtures into which lightstones had been placed for illumination. Their soft, bluish glow added a feel of winter to the hall. Shortly, Bryndís opened another door, carved with vines and trees, to let them into a smallish, round chamber that Magnús had never seen before.

Here, the walls were decorated with filigrees of silver. A gentle, dripping noise echoed from somewhere. Sunstones had been placed such that their glow sparked interesting patterns and reflections off the walls. In the center of the room was a stone pool. Its lip stood a few feet above the floor, and a platform jutted over the water at one side. Looking up, Magnús saw that the ceiling continued the interwoven pattern of silver and sunstones.

"It's the roots of a tree," Ólafur said beside him, delight in his voice as he traced the design with his eyes.

The scintillating light of the sunstones made it appear to Magnús that the carved vines were moving slightly. He felt an odd pull to his magic; the room somehow felt connected to the Hidden Ways he walked.

"Yggdrasill," Bryndís said, answering the unspoken question. "We gather at one of the roots of the World Tree, where that which separates Miðgarður from Álfheimur and from Ásgarður is thin."

She glided to the side of the pool where the platform began and gestured for Diwata to join her. "Child, sit here, above the waters of the pool. Gather yourself and begin your witchcraft. If the future refuses to reveal its face to you, I will seek repayment of the favor from Skuld."

Diwata hesitated, her hands against the waist of her shirt where an object was concealed. After a long moment, she sighed and withdrew a leather-bound notebook, green in color, its cover marked with runes that Magnús didn't recognize. She clutched it tightly in her hands until Bryndís said, "You have my oath, child. No huldufólk will attempt to take your grimoire."

Then Magnús understood. Unlike elves with their ability to draw on the magic of Álfheimur, humans used formulae, rituals and incantations to work their witchcraft. Their collections were recorded in grimoires like the one Diwata clutched. Karl's father was extremely possessive of his own book of spells, refusing to let even Karl touch it. In a rough voice, he'd told them how a witch searched and studied his life long for spells to add to his grimoire, before finally passing it on his death to the son with the most aptitude for witchcraft.

Diwata was the only female witch Magnús had encountered in decades; perhaps her father had no male children?

The baker clambered up onto the platform at the edge of the stone pool, then folded her legs to sink down, arranging herself with her grimoire open on her lap. She looked around as if unsettled, a small frown on her lips. Closing her eyes, the witch rocked slightly, then leaned in different directions. Eyes still shut, she shifted her seat around, turned her upper body slightly, shifted more. Finally, she sighed happily and came to stillness, as the glow from the sunstones on the walls brightened.

"Yes, you have it, child," Bryndís said. "You are aligned now with the magic of three Realms. Begin your spell."

Diwata opened her eyes and stared intently at the grimoire. She leaned toward the water to wet her hand, then traced runes on the stone platform, checking against the picture in the book. She murmured some quiet words, then said more loudly, "Weavers of fate, I seek your guidance."

The waters of the pool stirred and rippled, as if a breeze rushed over it, though the chamber was still. The scent of water in the air grew more pronounced, and pressure increased behind Magnús's eyes as if a rainstorm were on its way.

Diwata spoke on, her voice increasingly dreamy. "Urður, Verðandi, and Skuld, you whose arrival ended the days of bliss and ignorance for the gods, will you give your daughter the gift of what-is-to-come?"

The surface of the pool swirled, then darkened. Light flashed and dimmed within the water, and Magnús watched an image form of a man silhouetted on a hill, backlit by a monster of fire. Elves and humans died at the will of this man. At his feet, Magnús could now see, lay a shape like a dead falcon. Its plumage was golden and brown, quite unlike the white and gray of an Icelandic gyrfalcon. Somehow Magnús knew it was a human, and male.

Diwata moaned, drawing his gaze. Sweat darkened her hair now, plastering black strands to her face. Light gleamed down from the sunstones and up from the pool, leaving patterns and glowing whorls on her skin and tee-shirt.

"I can't find the Falcon," she said, voice tense. "I'm trying, but sorcery surrounds him." She rocked some more, straining.

"Easy, child," Bryndís said. "Let the Nornir guide you; do not work against them."

Ólafur's boots scuffed on stone as he moved closer to the platform where Diwata struggled silently. "Dee, what if you try a different approach? If you can't see the Falcon directly, can you see if Magnús will find him in time?"

Diwata's head whipped around to pin Magnús. Her eyes were completely white, as if she had been struck blind. Panic twisted her features as she opened her mouth, but the voice that emerged was not of Miðgarður or Álfheimur. Ringing tones declaimed a new prophecy.

"—*Before the sun rises today, the Falcon will alight on the arm of Magnús. He will lead Magnús to the Black Priest and into mortal peril. If the Falcon dies, Iceland dies. Yet if the Falcon lives, Magnús will meet his doom.*—"

Magnús blinked several times, stunned and silent. *His doom…* Huldufólk lived centuries, barring disaster. Bryndís herself had watched Vikings arrive on the shores of Iceland, more than a thousand years earlier. Was Magnús to see his own life thread cut short?

His gaze shifted rapidly among random spots on the walls of the room. He was unable to focus, feeling as if a spotlight shone too brightly on his head. Diwata seemed almost embarrassed, either *for* him or for having been the one to pronounce his doom. Ólafur looked shocked.

Logically, Magnús could just avoid this Falcon person entirely, find someone else willing to track him down and thwart the prophecy. Who would he call on, though?

Bryndís regarded him coolly. Her clear gaze told Magnús that she followed the track of his thoughts, confirmed when she answered his unspoken doubts.

"Somehow, my son, you have drawn the attention of the gods. I believe your path was set after the death of Sigurjón, when you asked Queen Hildur for her blessing to protect other humans. Now you must follow your calling to the ends of fate."

Magnús stiffened in anger and a touch of shame that Bryndís

knew he was looking for a way out of the prophecy. Churlishly, he said, "You could show some regret that I've just received a death sentence. My *mother*."

The pause was intended to hurt, but Bryndís never flinched. Her voice, though, was softer when she spoke again.

"This task is set for you, whether by the Nornir, the Æsir, or some power unknown to me. My son, never doubt that I am proud of the work you have done. You have always been drawn to the mortal world, but after Sigurjón, you set yourself upon a new path. Protector of humans in Iceland."

She leaned toward him, and her voice rang with authority. "I hear in this prophecy the fulfillment of all you have been driven to achieve since your beloved died one hundred years ago. This vision portends a threat to humans and huldufólk alike."

Magnús slumped back heavily against one of the filigreed walls, then slid to sit on the floor. Bryndís had a point. His failure to protect Sigurjón from elven malice or mischief still hurt all these decades on.

Magnús foresaw then the abyss that could swallow both his people and the humans if left uncurbed. That was why he had asked Queen Hildur for her imprimatur to protect humans and to bring justice in matters involving magical threats. The missing hikers alone proved that danger, and trolls were not the only threat.

But buoyed by their faith in the land wights, huldufólk generally avoided the affairs of humans, unless something directly threatened one of the elf-towns. They trusted the Landvættir to protect them from external threats and otherwise kept to their own society. So he had virtually no other elf to whom he could pass this burden.

Anyway, Diwata's prophecy seemed to say that their land's only hope lay in *Magnús* forging ahead and guarding this Falcon himself.

Ólafur spoke up cautiously. "Prophecies can be misinterpreted or even beaten. It's the only future Dee can see, but that doesn't mean another seer—"

Diwata interrupted angrily. "That vision I just received is the most wonderful, magical thing that has ever happened to me. There's no way another seer could achieve a more direct connection to the Nornir."

Bryndís lifted a hand slightly, and silence fell. She gathered her robe around herself, the weird lights of the room glistening against her golden head. "We must divide this problem into tasks. I will contact Queen Hildur with the news and also seclude myself to review my memories for why those terms—the Black Priest, the Bishop's Shackles—stirred something. Diwata, child, I'm sure you are aware of the...strain between our people and the witches council. I would ask you to examine any records preserved by the council for relevant history."

Diwata's jaw took on a determined set. "The jerks sitting on the council will resist sharing."

"I don't know this story," Ólafur said, looking puzzled. "Why is there trouble between us?"

Diwata said, "As I heard it, the troll uprising happened in, uh, I don't remember the year. The end of the thirteen hundreds, anyway. Witches aligned with the elves, the dwarves, and a few other races to push back the trolls. Then a few of the witches got greedy. They stole some of the magic used by the huldufólk and the dvergar, but they didn't know what they were doing. The forces they drew upon triggered a massive volcanic eruption."

"That was the Öræfajökull eruption," Magnús added. "Something like a third of the country was buried under gravel."

"That wasn't just gravel, it was troll pieces, too," Diwata said, her voice grim. "Lots of deaths, lots of finger-pointing. Things were always strained after that. Even now, those assho—uh, bozos on the council don't trust the huldufólk." She shot a grimace toward Bryndís. "But I'll get the records somehow."

"I have no doubt," Bryndís said with a gentle nod. "Magnús, the arrival of the Falcon is imminent."

"I understand, there's a falcon arriving by airplane, and I'm supposed to meet him. But how? Something like four million humans a year fly to Iceland. I'll never be able to identify one threat out of such a volume."

Ólafur said, "Diwata's prophecy sounded pretty definitive to me. Somehow, you'll just know the Falcon, and before sunrise."

"Okay, optimist," Magnús said, stretching up a hand for Ólafur to help him to his feet. "I'll worry about the stinger in that definitive prophecy's tail later. If the threat is so severe that the entire country may be threatened"—Diwata squawked, but Magnús barreled on—"*and* I agree it is, I have to act now. It's almost four o'clock. On the faith our interpretation is right, I'm going to head to the Keflavik airport since that's the only one with international arrivals. Can you find out what flights are scheduled to land before the sun rises?"

"You want Diwata to scry for arrival times?" Ólafur sounded incredulous.

"No, Cousin. I want you to use the Internet."

EIGHT

A few hours later, Magnús paced through the Arrivals terminal of Keflavik, scanning the tourists arriving for Reykjavik. Ólafur had identified only two flights still due from the west before sunrise that morning, predicted for a quarter past six.

Magnús had no trouble slipping through security checkpoints so he could wait near a gate—invisibility had its benefits. Based on his inexplicable intuition that the Falcon was human and male, his best course was to approach every male passenger that emerged. If Ólafur was right, Magnús could somehow identify this Falcon who was either to die or be his doom.

The thought made his guts tighten. As lonely as his chosen life could be at times, Magnús was not ready to leave it behind. And yet...

Immortality. All the huldufólk he knew embraced their long lives. They seemed content to measure time by geological calendars—the growth of trees, the eruptions of lava, the advance and retreat of glaciers. Other than the very few elves who died from violence or misfortune, when huldufólk eventually grew tired of life in Miðgarður, they returned to Álfheimur. They became fully part of the ljósálfar, the light elves, embracing a world of scintillating but unchanging beauty.

Bryndís was right, though; Magnús had always been different. The span of centuries interested him less than the speed with which mortals grew and innovated and changed. He loved humans precisely because they saw the magic in a sunset every day. They lived such short periods of time, and their years passed quickly enough that they felt obligated to celebrate each turn of a season.

Already in his four hundred years, he had seen friends grow from childhood, to maturity, to old age and death. Karl, the human he was closest to, was the great-grandson of someone Magnús had skied with in the early nineteen hundreds, as mortals counted time. How many more friends would he watch age and die? Even if Sigurjón had lived, they would have had no more than fifty or sixty years together, a mere blink for someone like his mother.

Magnús wondered, in quiet moments, why he had really taken on the thankless job of protecting humans from threats like trolls and even cruelly mischievous elves like Lars. It wasn't about keeping going, about moving beyond the loneliness his lifespan gave him. No, he cared about these mortals. Iceland was as much their home as his.

But maybe, somewhere deep inside, Magnús wondered. If he died while on Miðgarður, might he be reunited with Sigurjón?

His doom—

The earlier of his two targeted flights arrived from Vancouver. Magnús moved among the passengers, slipping smoothly and invisibly, looking into the eyes of each man and boy. He let his awareness grow. He couldn't read their minds as easily as Ólafur, but he tried to feel for anything *different* about one of them.

Something that might signal a supernatural threat. Yet nothing stirred his senses, magical or otherwise.

If he missed the Falcon at this point... The images from Diwata's vision tortured his memories. He saw again huldufólk dying as they fought, struck by lightning and bullets and fire. The catastrophe ushered in by the unknown man in the black-brimmed hat, chaining a creature that then killed at his command. The dead body of a falcon that wasn't a falcon at all, but a human whose very fate was in Magnús's hands...

Somehow, that memory was the most horrifying of all. Magnús would fail and this special being marked by the gods would die. And with the Falcon's death, the entire country would fall to the evil of some Black Priest and his army.

Magnús tapped his foot anxiously on the floor of the Arrivals corridor as he waited for the crew to disembark as well. The male captain and a male attendant passed by him, still causing no unusual feeling.

About to move on, Magnús stopped abruptly as the terminal suddenly blurred. Karl was writing on the mirror Magnús had enchanted for him. Unseen by humans, golden letters flared in the air, just long enough for Magnús to read:

3 more grps missing last 2 weeks, no trace, list in usual spot

Damn this prophecy. Magnús should be looking into the disappearances, find out if trolls were involved, see if he could save anyone. But here he was, a pebble in a stream of humanity, a tool of fate, hoping to find one particular man amidst a sea of travelers. He ran fingers through his hair in frustration.

Cursing silently, he hurried to meet the flight from Boston, past huge posters of the Blue Lagoon, of puffins and whales, of an erupting volcano. Where was the damned gate?

He followed posted numbers, moving faster as he dodged around slow-moving travelers, an elderly man being pushed in a wheelchair, a tired mother trying to corral three young children....

It seemed to take forever to navigate the airport, this peculiar human construct.

By the time Magnús made it to the correct gate, passengers had already begun to stream off and toward passport control. Had he already missed the Falcon? With a growing sense of urgency, he darted among the mass of travelers, looking into their eyes, hoping for some echo of warning. Still nothing. And only a few days to the new moon, when the invasion would be set in motion.

Just a handful of passengers straggled down the ramp from airplane to terminal now, and Magnús cursed again. His plan had been all wrong. What else could he do to find the Falcon? Maybe this approach made no sense, wandering aimlessly through crowds of humans—

"Oh, I'm sorry!"

Startled, Magnús realized that someone had walked right into him, jarring his arm. Automatically, he reached out a steadying hand to the shoulder of the person who'd bumped into him.

The young man before Magnús was small, perhaps no more than five foot seven, and very thin. The boney shoulder under his puffy red jacket suggested delicacy. Ruddy skin on a handsome face might mean a lot of time spent outdoors. His hair was reddish-brown, and his eyes were such a light brown they might have been golden.

The young man stared up at Magnús in confusion. "I'm so sorry," he blurted again in English, stepping back. "Did I hurt you? Step on your foot?"

Magnús almost shook his head, but then realization crashed over him. He froze, narrowing his gaze at the man before him. The man who'd bumped into him, when Magnús had effortlessly evaded all other humans. The man who saw him, even though Magnús had not consciously made himself visible.

In his memory, Diwata—or the entity speaking through her— was saying, "The Falcon will alight on the arm of Magnús."

He let his awareness of the traveler grow, pouring himself into those golden-brown eyes that looked up guilelessly. Something familiar drifted there, behind his eyes. It was as if—

Could this young man have huldufólk blood in him?

Magnús carefully brushed across surface thoughts. Even when humans were hard for him to "hear," usually he could at least sense their strongest emotions. Certainly, he felt curiosity, nervousness, and even desire coming from the young man's mind.

Desire? Interesting, but for later.

He concentrated more. Surprisingly, there were concepts there, too, becoming clearer. *Homesick. Obligation. Why did I agree to come here? Do I have my passport?*

And there was a name, too, adrift in the young man's mind. Alastair? No, not quite. It was...

"Altair Fálkason," Magnús said aloud.

So. That was the name of the Falcon. The name of his doom.

CHAPTER

NINE

Altair stared up at the hot man he'd walked into like a dweeb. The stranger was youngish, probably just a few years older than his own twenty-three. His pale, narrow face was beautiful, almost radiant. Silver-blond hair shimmered in the lights of the airport. The guy stood at least seven or eight inches taller than Altair, his lean frame showing off the snug sky-blue sweater and leg-hugging black pants that he wore. A snack, Jason would call him.

One hand on Altair's shoulders as if to steady himself, the snack's ice-blue eyes glittered down. Was that annoyance, or amusement? Those eyes narrowed.

A curious sensation tickled behind Altair's ear. As the man's eyes flicked over him, something like a cool breeze stirred, but it was inside Altair's head rather than on his face. That breeze carried with it the idea of ancient snow, of glaciers carving the land over millennia, of long-vanished forests. There was the sound of creaking ice, and words on the breeze... Words he could almost make out if he had time. If he just knew how to *listen*—

"Altair Fálkason," the stranger said slowly, in a resonant bari-

57

tone that sent a shiver down Altair's back. It startled away the strange idea drifting across the surface of Altair's mind.

"That's, uh, that's me," he stammered.

The man said nothing else but continued to stare down intently. It was alarming, to be honest. Was the dude mad at him for being a klutz? Altair wasn't used to being noticed by a handsome man, let alone studied. And by someone who knew his name. Which was also odd, so maybe...?

"Did the university arrange for you to meet me and bring me to Reykjavik?" Altair asked.

The hot stranger hesitated but nodded, slowly at first, then with determination. "Exactly," he said. "I'm called Magnús. The university hired me to take you to your hotel."

His English seemed flawless, but a slight accent, the curious way he rounded his vowels, struck Altair as musical. "Nice to meet you," he said cautiously, feeling that this Magnús wasn't exactly thrilled with the driving assignment.

Altair extended the hand not holding his luggage, only to realize he still clutched his passport and entry card. Before he could transfer them to shake with Magnús, the tall man turned to start walking in the direction the other passengers had taken.

"Come along. As soon as you're cleared to enter the country, we'll be on our way."

Altair hesitated, nonplussed at the abruptness. Sure, the guy was sex on legs, but maybe a bit of a tool, too? He shrugged and trailed behind Magnús through the airport, weary from his flight, already wishing he were back in Boston.

Abruptly, Magnús pointed and said, "Passport control is there. I'll be waiting for you when you come out into the main terminal. Do you have any other luggage?"

"No," Altair said, hearing his voice crack with fatigue. He hefted the patched suitcase and satchel he'd carried onto the plane. "I only brought these. I figured with all the traveling I'm scheduled for, it would be better to pack light." He glanced down at the passport and card still clutched in his hand. "I hope I have everything. I've never been out of the States before."

Magnús shrugged. "Entry is usually quick and easy. I'll see you soon."

He sauntered away, and Altair sighed. *Tool-ish for sure.* And was it weird that a hired driver could come right into the terminal? In the States, he was pretty sure a driver would have had to wait on the other side of security.

Oh well, things were probably very different in Iceland. He tried to see where Magnús had gone, but there was no glimpse of him.

The passport line did move quickly at least. In just minutes, Altair stepped to a window, where he handed his travel documents to a uniformed woman. His shoulders felt like they were up at his ears. *Did I forget anything?* When the agent didn't ask for any other papers, he released the breath he'd been holding.

Flipping quickly through the blue passport booklet, the agent asked in accented English, "Purpose of your visit?"

"I'm here as a graduate student, working on a project for my university—"

"How long will you be staying in Iceland?" she interrupted, her tone bored.

"Two weeks. It could have been longer, but I need to get home—"

"Where are you staying?"

"Um, in Reykjavik at first. I think it's called the Hotel Cabin. In two days, I'm heading to other parts of Iceland to tour various power plants. I can check my itinerary if you need the details."

"No need." Apparently satisfied, she stamped his passport, returned it to him, and that seemed to be all. He hesitated for a moment to be sure, long enough that she jerked her head sharply at him to move on.

"Okay," he muttered. "Geez."

So maybe all Icelanders were cold and abrupt, not just Magnús.

Another wave of homesickness hit as he walked away, like when he had looked out the plane window as they were landing. The flat, treeless landscape of Iceland below had struck him as alien. Forbidding.

Altair *so* didn't belong in this place. His studies, his work, his family, his cramped bedroom even—they all seemed so far away. If he didn't fear that Uncle Trausti would cut him off if he didn't get his head out of his ass and finish his thesis, he never would have accepted this grant.

With a sigh, Altair followed signs past the baggage claim and Customs areas until he emerged through a double door into the main terminal. Several people clustered nearby, hugging other passengers or holding up signs of a livery or tour company.

Magnús raised a hand where he stood at a slight distance from the throng: solitary, tall, and glittering in the bright lights of the main terminal. Altair had been prepared to use some of his meager grant funds to pay for a bus ride into Reykjavik, so the gift of a driver was a relief.

"Well, that was easy," he murmured as he joined Magnús.

Magnús merely nodded, turned, and walked away toward the airport exit sign.

The cold that greeted Altair as they stepped outside made him shiver. He could see his breath in the frigid morning air. In Boston, the spring flowers were starting to bloom. This weather, though, felt like winter was still upon Iceland. His sweater and down-filled coat protected him, but his face and hands immediately felt the chill.

Argh. What was he doing here, in this frigid country?

Unmoored—that was the word for how he felt. Just like those first few months in the orphanage after Mom died, and then every time he'd shifted to a different foster home. So many goodbyes, to caretakers and to kids, his foster siblings. So many different beds.

His legs worked fast as he tried to match Magnús's long stride to the parking lot. Cars bore thin layers of frost on their windows that glittered in the morning sun. At least the fast pace was warming him up. Altair found himself babbling to keep his fears at bay.

"I kind of expected to be interrogated and searched for contraband, like in the movies. You know? Shown into a dingy room, lights shining in my eyes. 'Do you have anything to declare?' bellowed at me—"

"And do you?" Magnús asked sharply without looking back.

Altair faltered for a moment, surprised at the tone. "Well, no. I didn't bring anything with me. Except materials about the power plants I'm seeing."

"Power plants?" Magnús finally seemed to notice that Altair was struggling to keep up with him and extended a hand to take Altair's carry-on suitcase. The guy acted completely unfazed by the chilly air, though he wore no coat over his sweater. So unfair— handsome *and* immune to the arctic blast that apparently passed as spring in this country.

"Didn't the university mention, when they hired you to pick me up?" Altair asked. "I'm here on a grant to study a series of geothermal and hydroelectric facilities..."

He knew he was nattering on, but he didn't care. Talking distracted him from shivering as he followed Magnús through a parking area and to a bright yellow van that seemed tiny next to Magnús's height. It looked like a compressed station wagon, with a boxy back end that apparently served for storage.

"It's so cute!" Altair gushed and then hated himself for it. "Um, what is it?"

Magnús glanced at him; he might have had a barely-there smile. "It's a Renault Kangoo. Last year's model."

"How's its fuel efficiency? I've heard gas prices in Iceland are high."

"...Good? I think." For the first time, Magnús looked less than sure of himself, which puzzled Altair. He'd have assumed a professional driver should be a car guy and know his own vehicle's gas consumption.

Magnús opened the back of the Kangoo to store Altair's suitcase, then held out a hand for the satchel. Altair hesitated, but he wasn't sure why. Awkwardly, he slipped the strap over his head and passed the black nylon bag to Magnús.

As soon as Magnús took it, his eyes widened, then narrowed to a grimace. He crooked his head at the satchel.

"What do you have in here?" he asked, suspicion shading his deep voice as he gingerly placed the bag on the floor of the van.

The tone made something in Altair defensive. "Nothing much. The materials I mentioned about power plants. I put them all into a binder to keep them organized. My laptop, e-reader, chargers. That's it, really."

"Hm," Magnús muttered as he opened the passenger-side door for Altair. What momentary friendliness or humor he had shown was gone again.

As Altair strapped himself into the seat, Magnús leaned against the open passenger door, staring down with a strange intensity in those blue eyes. Altair again heard the ghost of an icy whisper across his brain, felt a slight itch behind his ear, and raised a hand to rub it.

Magnús's gaze shifted to Altair's ear, and his scowl deepened. "Is there something wrong? You winced suddenly."

"Did I? No, nothing's wrong. I just got this peculiar feeling in my head. A few times now, since we met in the terminal. And I've got this tickle, almost like someone's brushing me with a feather." Altair's face warmed; he probably sounded ridiculous. "I'm just tired from the long flight."

Magnús cocked his own head and stared at him for another moment, then closed the door and came around to the driver's side. Taking his place behind the wheel, he stated, "You are staying at the Hotel Cabin."

"That's right. I can look up the address if you need—"

"I know where it is."

They began the drive in silence. Altair, drowning in exhaustion and loneliness, sagged into his seat. Here he was, thousands of miles from Boston, with no one to talk to except Mister Tall, Pale, and Handsome, who clearly wasn't interested in conversation.

At least the car warmed up quickly.

TEN

Altair stared wide-eyed through the windshield as the car exited the airport. Magnús drove eastward along a straight highway that cut across the severe, rock-strewn landscape. The sun just topped the horizon on this morning in late April, bathing everything Altair could see in golden-red tones. Flat land, riddled with small rock formations, stretched in all directions. Frost glistened on the rocks like diamond dust. On one side of the highway, the airport's runways seemed out of place, as if embossed on the forbidding landscape. The lack of trees or even shrubbery seemed alarming, compared to the lushness he was used to in Boston. Sharp, black shadows lay curiously on the lava fields. Almost lunar in its starkness, the play of light and dark over the land was startling. Unnerving, actually.

It was all so unfamiliar, so different from the tree-lined streets of Cambridge, or the neat lawns of the Boston Common. Another wave of homesickness and exhaustion made his eyes prickle.

Altair blinked away the momentary weakness because, yes, there was beauty out there, too. Reluctantly, he admitted to himself that he wanted to feel that ground beneath his feet. His engineering studies drew him to wind farms and turbines, but his professor had encouraged Altair to apply for this grant to study the marvels hidden beneath the severe surface of Iceland, or shaping its surface. Rumbling volcanos, geothermal springs, icy winds whistling down from snowcapped peaks... So much raw power waiting to be harnessed.

Two weeks. That was all. He'd study the various power plants on his itinerary in depth, applying as many of their wonders and techniques as he could to further his own work. Then he could go home to Boston, to the family reminding him in various ways that his time was running out.

They were right, of course. He needed to buckle down. If he didn't complete this tour, he'd find himself jobless and homeless, with nowhere to go, and no family...

Magnús's voice woke Altair from a near doze. "Tell me more about your studies."

"Huh?" Altair jerked a bit, then realized he'd been dreaming. "Oh. Right." He yawned widely and shook off his feeling of dread. Surprisingly, he felt a grin start to form. "I was dying to talk to someone about this all through the flight, and now you're trapped with me."

The corner of Magnús's mouth quirked up. He murmured, "It's fortunate for me, then, that the drive is less than one hour."

Encouraged by the humor, no matter how slight, Altair soared into a discussion of his passion. "I'm an engineering student, right? I'm working on my dissertation about efficient and sustainable ways to harness natural resources."

"Very nice," Magnús grunted. "Why come to Iceland?"

"Well, you probably know that Iceland is a world leader in renewable energy. Wind turbines are my main focus, and Iceland doesn't have many large-scale programs of those yet. But hydro-electricity? Geothermal heat pumps? This country is a huge innovator. My advisor convinced me this is the best place to study those designs and then apply them to my own proposals."

Magnús nodded but offered no comment. Altair kept chattering about his ideas until he noticed they were driving into a good-sized city.

"Is this Reykjavik?"

Magnús shrugged. "One of its outskirts. We'll be in the city proper and at your hotel in about twenty more minutes."

They passed a pillar that contained an interesting symbol. In the center was the blue flag Altair recognized as Iceland's, with its cross of red and white. But around the flag were four figures; they seemed to be a man, a bull, a dragon, and a bird of some kind.

"What's that symbol for?" he asked, pointing.

"It's the coat of arms of Iceland," Magnús said. "The four figures represent the Landvættir. The word means, oh, land wights in English."

"Land wights. I've never heard that phrase."

"Do you want to hear about them? Very well. Well, legend has it that Iceland is protected by four guardian wights or spirits at the cardinal points. Fearsome Dreki the Dragon guards the Eastern shore. Mighty Bergrisi the Giant stands watch in the South. The Bull Griðungur roams in the West, and high-flying Gammur the Eagle protects the North."

"Protect from what?"

"From sorcerers." Magnús's tone was flat and factual, as if he believed in the fairy tale.

"Um, sorcery?"

"Oh yes. Hundreds of years ago, the king of Denmark and Norway desired to conquer Iceland. He sent his most powerful sorcerer to assess the country's defenses—"

"Sent by boat, or by longship, I guess they're called?"

"Do you want to hear this story or not?" Magnús asked with a scowl.

"Sorry, I'll shut up. Go on, a Norwegian sorcerer…"

Magnús waited a beat, apparently testing to make sure Altair was going to listen, then continued.

"This king knew that Iceland was protected by hidden folk and magical creatures, so he needed his sorcerer to find a way past them all. Well, the sorcerer turned himself into a whale. After swimming around at a distance, he grew chilly in the cold water, so he approached Iceland's fjords on the west coast. He swam close to land and prepared to regain his human form.

"Suddenly, an enormous bull with curving, golden horns charged from the woods and into the water's edge. It bellowed its challenge, and other land spirits swarmed to help it drive away the sorcerer. He knew he couldn't come ashore there and swam away quickly. There was no way his king could invade from the west—"

"I didn't know Iceland had bulls. Sorry, shutting up." Altair mimed zipping his mouth closed, gratified at the twitch of Magnús's full lips.

"He went south around Iceland," Magnús continued. "Again, the sorcerer swam toward land. This time, he became a human and stood on the rocky beach. He rubbed his hands gleefully, thinking he had found the way in that his king wanted. But the ground rumbled and shook. A mountain giant came into sight, running at the sorcerer, its enormous club held high. With a terrified scream, the sorcerer dove back into the water and became a whale again."

Magnús grew more animated as he talked. Altair was caught up in the absurd account in spite of himself, both for the legend and its teller. "This is a great story," he said, grinning. "Why hasn't Disney made a movie about it?"

"I'm not finished," Magnús said sternly, and Altair held up his hands in an apology. "The sorcerer continued his way around the island until he approached what we now call Egilsstaðir—"

"That's on my itinerary! Well, I think so. I didn't realize that was how you say it. A-yil-sta-thir. I'm sorry, I don't know any words in Icelandic, and a lot of the names seem very hard to pronounce."

Magnús met his eyes this time, a slight curve easing the severity of his mouth. "I understand. I sometimes think the hu—that *we* delight in making the language barrier as high as possible to show independence from the rest of Europe. Now, do you want me to finish the story?"

"Yes, please." Altair tried to sound meek and apologetic.

"Fine. As the sorcerer swam to shore, a huge dragon flew at him from the nearest mountain, and with the dragon came hundreds, no, thousands, of snakes, lizards, and scaly things as well. Sea serpents rose around the transfigured whale, too."

"Gross, but dope, too. My money is on Team Dragon," Altair said with a slight chuckle.

Magnús seemed to be holding back a laugh, too, as he continued. "So. Exhausted by the long swim, and terrified of the great protectors he had seen, the sorcerer headed to the North. Iciest, coldest, most remote—he guessed it would be the easiest point for the king to attack."

"Wrong!"

"Exactly. This time, a mighty eagle appeared in the sky as the whale approached. It dove at him, accompanied by thousands of birds of all kinds. The eagle's talons scored the whale's flesh, the birds pecked at his skin and eyes. The sorcerer turned away and dove deep to escape the torment. He swam and swam all the way back to tell the king that Iceland was guarded by fierce creatures, and there was no way past them. And ever since, Iceland has known it is protected by the Landvættir from sorcerous invasion."

"That's a great story. And it's fascinating that those figures are on the coat of arms," Altair said, smiling. "All these centuries and the country still pretends it's got these protectors."

Magnús gave him a sharp look. "Be careful where you call the

Landvættir 'pretend.' There are many who still believe in the guardian wights." His voice was tight.

"Are you kidding me?" Altair asked, his brow furrowing. "In this day and age?"

"Wights, trolls, witches, ghosts." Magnús paused, then added, "Elves. You'll find as you visit this country that we hold our folktales close to our heart, and it would be unwise to mock."

Altair didn't know how to respond to that, or to the edge he picked up in the driver's tone. *Man, this guy runs hot and cold*, he thought privately as he sat back and looked at the city they were passing through.

It was modern, and the buildings seemed to be tightly clustered. The view was nothing like the congested skyline of home. One- and two-story houses, clad in what looked like corrugated tin siding, were painted in blocks of colors: red, blue and yellow. The structures gradually grew taller, maybe apartments, he guessed, with a few taller buildings poking up here and there. Offices perhaps? In the center of town, an enormous white building rose, shining in the morning sunlight like a monolith or church tower—

"That's Hallgrímskirkja," Magnús volunteered, gesturing at the edifice Altair spied. "The tallest church in Iceland."

Altair mouthed the strange word to himself. "Hall-grims-keer-ka. I'm kind of worried that with the way I say things here, I'm going to start an international incident."

"Words have power. Especially in Iceland."

"Why especially?"

Magnús only shook his head. "It's just something we say. Now, here we are, at your hotel."

Feeling that Magnús was deliberately evading his question, Altair looked up at the façade of a mid-rise, boxy building. It seemed a nice place, not flashy or huge, but neat-looking. His grant left no room for luxury, so he'd taken a chance and booked an economy hotel. The sight was reassuringly pleasant. As he studied it, again that tickle brushed his ear.

Magnús said, "So. I'll be back to pick you up at two o'clock this afternoon, if that's not too much for you with the time zone change."

Altair whirled in surprise to look at him. "Pick me up? For what?"

"To show you the sights of Reykjavik."

Guilt gnawed a bit at Altair. Willa had warned him that he had no time for sightseeing, that he should get right to work and prepare for his meetings at the university. But Jason had encouraged him to sightsee, and when would he ever be in Iceland again? Plus, Magnús was really nice to look at, even if he was a tool.

"Well, uh, it's really nice the university hired you to do that. Thank you."

So Altair would work a bit until two o'clock, and more after they finished sightseeing. According to the clock on the dash of the car, it was almost seven thirty in the morning, local time, and Altair tried to do the math. Probably about two thirty in the morning back in Boston, and he hadn't had dinner or breakfast on the plane.

"There's a restaurant in your hotel," Magnús volunteered, his voice as tight as when they began the ride. "Or if you walk a few blocks in that direction"—he gestured—"you'll find several places to eat."

Altair felt he'd insulted Magnús somehow, but he wasn't sure what he'd done or said wrong.

Magnús got out to retrieve Altair's luggage. He handed over the carry-on but hesitated before releasing the satchel. Ice-blue eyes again on Altair's, he asked, "Do you have any questions for me before I go?"

"No, I think I'm set. I'll get checked in, eat something, call my friends, and try to get some work done. Maybe catch a short nap before we head back out."

"Good. This afternoon, then." Magnús climbed back in his Kangoo and drove away.

Feeling a little empty and strangely bereft, Altair watched the car disappear. There was something about that man that drew Altair to him. Good looks, obviously, but it was more than that.

He had the oddest sensation that Magnús could keep him safe. But safe from what?

ELEVEN

Seething, Magnús drove his borrowed Kangoo by Karl's home. That little, young.... Altair had mocked the Landvættir, scoffing at the wights and the rest.

"Pretend," Magnús muttered savagely. He was used to encountering Icelanders who knew and believed, at least to some extent, in the supernatural world around them. And of course the First Covenant prevented Magnús from proving to Altair that the Landvættir still guarded Iceland. But this tourist's skepticism and...and *mockery* were just infuriating.

"Oh yes, the human civilization here is, what, five times as old as his country? Huldufólk were in Iceland before Vikings ever touched the shore of North America. Yet how quaint that we 'pretend.'"

And *this* was a human he was supposed to protect. A talkative, inexperienced young man who studied power plants, of all things.

A quiet part of Magnús's mind reminded him, *He did see the beauty in Iceland. After a while. And not all humans here believe in the Landvættir and the rest.*

Sigurjón hadn't believed the stories were true either, at first.

Magnús smiled at the memory of Sigurjón's face, when the elf deliberately vanished in front of him. Sigurjón had been excited and intrigued, though, rather than scared. Magnús remembered standing still while Sigurjón ran a light finger over his pointed ears, through his silky hair that was just enough different from human hair to be noticeable at a touch. The young human put his hands to his mouth, laughing delightedly when he realized Magnús was not lying to him about being one of the huldufólk.

Magnús snorted dismissively. Altair's surface thoughts had been oddly easy to pick up. The human preferred his common Boston greenery and trees, his family...

Strange, though. Altair's thoughts about his family were odd. Full of longing and tension. Dread of being replaced or pushed away. And there was something unnerving in his satchel, though Magnús found nothing in Altair's mind about the Black Priest, the Falcon, or the Bishop's Shackles.

Maybe Ólafur would be able to go deeper. Bryndís, as gyðja, should decide if that was an ethical use of Ólafur's gift; Magnús made a mental note to raise the issue with her.

He pulled to the curb at Karl's house. In a corner of his friend's garden, a small statue of a bearded man in a blue coat and tall red hat grinned cheekily. Magnús rolled his eyes at the joke: one of those ceramic garden gnomes humans thought were cute. Of all things to use as a message drop with an elf.

Besides, the statue looked nothing like a real gnome.

He turned the figure over and pulled a rolled-up paper from its hollow interior. A quick glance revealed the names, nationalities, travel dates, and last known locations of three parties of hikers that had vanished within the past month and still hadn't been found. All came from outside Iceland, Magnús noted. He needed some quiet to study the details and figure out what to do next. The missing people might still be alive, if Magnús could find them in time.

If only he didn't also need to deal with that annoying Altair. But a message from the Nornir could not be ignored. Keeping Altair alive seemed tied to the fate of the entire country. Why his own fate had been tangled with Altair's was a mystery. Surely the Nornir could have picked someone better suited to preserve Altair's life than Magnús, who was apparently destined either to fail or to die in the saving.

As he dithered, a low-pitched rumble began. The ground made a sharp shake, which gave way to a brief rolling sensation. Magnús automatically set his feet; tremors were a frequent occurrence in Iceland. Though the frequency had seemingly increased lately. What with the newly active volcano on the Reykjanes peninsula and more quakes, it seemed the land might be preparing a tremendous display of power.

He should check with Karl to see if the human agencies that tracked such things were predicting a major event.

Unquieted, still wrestling with his choices, trying to see a way to turn Altair over to someone else so he could get back to the trolls, Magnús drove away. He returned the Kangoo to the area from which he'd borrowed it, on the outskirts of Reykjavik. The glyph he'd traced in road dust before taking the boxy yellow car still glistened, though only elf eyes would see it as it worked subtle magic to deter anyone else from parking there.

Altair's question about the Kangoo's fuel efficiency came to mind, further unsettling Magnús. Of course driving someone's car burned fuel, but he had no idea how much, or what it cost the owner. Refilling a gas tank wasn't something he normally thought about, any more than he'd thought about giving oats to a horse he borrowed back in the nineteen hundreds. Now, though, a tinge of guilt entered his mind.

Magnús snorted. *Why am I worrying about anything that human said?*

Nevertheless, he withdrew from his pocket a polished piece of pumice; carved onto the surface with precise, straight lines was a glyph: a symbol of protection. Turning it over in his hand, he considered, then nodded. That would do.

He murmured the words of a spell that reminded the stone of its proud origin in an Icelandic volcano. Briefly the etched lines flared to light, forming a mystical sigil of Meili, god of travel. Left in the car, the stone would keep it safe from dents, rust, even weather damage for a time. If the owner of the Kangoo was from Iceland and had been raised on the folklore of elves—and wasn't too modern to believe in such tales, that is—they should recognize a gift of thanks from one of the huldufólk.

Satisfied, Magnús left the carpark on foot and set his path for Hamarinn. For home. Instead of opening the Hidden Ways, he opted to walk so he could think.

He followed the main roadway for a time, then continued along a side street in a straight line even farther away from the city. Tightly clustered houses, plain and solid with brightly colorful roofs, grew sparser as he walked. He enjoyed the elements humans had used hundreds of years earlier in making their houses and shelters. From turf houses to the passage farmhouses they used to call "gangabær," to the gabled farmhouses, they kept their best ideas and moved them forward while honoring their traditions.

Altair would probably sneer at the construction. No doubt his American engineering was far superior to techniques that had persisted for hundreds of years.

Give him time, Magnús cautioned himself with a sigh. *The Nornir have woven our fates together. There must be a reason I am needed to keep him alive.*

Ólafur and the others were right—he needed to set aside his investigation into the trolls, at least until after the new moon and whatever encounter that presaged. If Magnús was still alive after that, well, he could pick up the trail.

In the meantime, he ought to let Karl know what was happening. Perhaps the SAR units could investigate, cautiously?

A small store caught his attention, so he slipped inside invisibly to find a phone in an empty back office. He had to think to recall how to work the old dial. It worked, finally, and he reached Karl on his mobile phone.

"Hæ, it's Magnús," he said at Karl's greeting. "I have some bad news that will affect the search." As succinctly as he could, he explained about the prophecy and his role. "My gyðja tells me that I must apply my time to this invasion, as the greater threat."

"Well," Karl muttered, "I see your chieftain's point. I always appreciate your help, but this is what we train to do, sort of. I'll find a way to recruit help from those most likely to avoid or survive a troll encounter. When I put together that list for you, I noticed many of the disappearances took place along the Northern ranges. Perhaps my boss will agree to let me take a small team up that way to look around."

"I'll be free again in a few days. Well, if we figure out how to avert this prophecy," Magnús said. "Try to stay alive and out of troll hands until then."

CHAPTER

TWELVE

Karl Bjarnason was fourteen when he met an elf for the first time.

He'd grown up knowing that the huldufólk were as much a part of Iceland as he was, of course. His father Bjarni was a witch, and he'd raised Karl on all the old stories.

"The signs are everywhere, if you know how to look," Bjarni had said, his slate-gray eyes glinting. "Watch for a farm that's more prosperous than its neighbors, or where sheep give more and better wool. The farmer will be someone who has done a good turn for an elf and been repaid. Find a boulder in the middle of a town, with the nearby roads and buildings all laid out strangely. Chances are, the road builders met the huldufólk in a dream and were warned not to disturb an elf-village."

And so Karl had looked dutifully when he was ten and eleven. What child wouldn't? By the time he was twelve, he'd begun to doubt Bjarni. The old man refused to show him any magic—said Karl didn't have a talent for it.

79

At thirteen, he was convinced the whole thing about elves and land wights and sorcerers was bullshit. He stopped looking, and he stopped asking Bjarni for stories. His cross-country skiing and snowboarding took up much of his time instead.

And Karl was good, good enough to compete in the Winter Games, up in Akureyri. The festival was only a month away, in March, when Karl decided on some extra training before dinner. By five thirty, night had fallen, but the Bláfjöll runs where he trained had electric lighting.

Board under his arm, ski boots on his feet, he trudged across the snow. Maybe his mind was too much on the competition, or on schoolwork, or on that CrossFit star he'd watched avidly on YouTube. In any event, he didn't realize he'd missed the right turning until he found himself on the back side of the practice hill.

Which would have been fine, except that as his eyes tracked up, up, up the massive snowpack...an earth tremor hit. The snowy face shifted, and then a sheet of it broke away, directly above where he stood. Gravity caught the sheet and began to pull.

The avalanche was so unexpected, so close, that all his training vanished from his head. Karl's heart plummeted. He stood paralyzed with shock in the face of approaching death.

"Your board," a voice said.

Karl had a moment to register a tall, thin man standing next to him, where a moment before he'd been alone. Silver-blond hair, too long to be fashionable, glistened around the stranger's head. Even in the dim light of the snowfield, the man's eyes shone, icy blue. He was objectively handsome, in a way that made Karl too aware of his own coarse features.

Impatiently, the stranger yanked Karl's snowboard from under his arm, threw it onto the snow, and then pulled Karl onto it. Reflexively, Karl locked his boots in place. The man put one foot on the surface of the board behind Karl's trailing boot and pushed hard with the other. Like a thing possessed, the snowboard took off.

The avalanche was almost upon them, its roar filling Karl's ears as he leaned into the run. Years of training took over. Karl flowed with the motion, smoothly gliding even with the unaccountable presence of the man behind him. Before he could make sense of that, he realized the board wasn't sliding *down* the hill, but straight across. Ice and snow and a sound like breaking thunder hit. Karl was sure the avalanche had him.

But the board was still moving. The snow sheet had passed him by, and he had lived. His knees suddenly failed and he went down, hearing a curse and shout from the stranger as they fell.

They lay tangled for a moment in the snow. Karl's boots were still locked into the board, but apparently, he'd taken no harm. He rolled his head and found the stranger standing up already, dusting snow off his too-thin pants.

The man crouched again to help Karl get out of the snowboard, then extended a hand to pull him to his feet.

A thousand stories collided in Karl's head, with about a million questions. When he opened his mouth, though, all that came out was a croak.

The stranger gave him a half smile. "I owed Bjarni a favor," he said in a melodic, low voice. "Please say Magnús sends Bjarni regards...and his son. The debt is paid."

Magnús winked, made as if to turn away, and vanished.

CHAPTER

THIRTEEN

Heart heavy as he worried about Karl and other rescue workers taking on trolls, Magnús returned to Hamarinn and to Bryndís's longhouse. He found her in the large chamber where they'd met before; Diwata and Ólafur had gone to deal with the witches council.

Seated beside his mother on a carved, oaken bench placed against one wall, he opened his thoughts and heart to her in the deep communion sacred to elves. In moments, she'd absorbed the details, from Magnús meeting Altair, to letting him off at his hotel.

He concluded silently, «Altair was surprisingly easy for me to read. As far as I could tell, he knows nothing of the Black Priest, the Falcon, the Bull, or the Bishop's Shackles.»

Bryndís nodded and spoke aloud. "He also seems unaware of potentially being elf-breed. It is an old story, actually. One of the huldufólk rashly falls in love with a human, perhaps even leaves Iceland, and bears or sires children. Over a few generations, the blood thins, but occasionally a descendant is born with a spark of our magic. You believe Altair is an orphan?"

"Yes, he was apparently raised in a series of foster homes, but he now has a family in Boston. Though the sense of family was... unsettled. Full of anxiety."

Bryndís gave him a wry look. "Family is complicated, whether human or huldufólk."

Magnús ignored the comment as another concern grabbed him. "He knew at some level that I was inside his mind, though he doesn't understand what that means."

"I have heard of humans with a touch of our mind-speech, or the ability to conceal themselves to some degree if they stand still. A few have enough magic to blunder into our elf-towns. I recall one human woman who could see us plainly, no matter how much we hid. Some believe that witches have elf-blood in them, and that is what allows them to tap into the land's power."

Magnús scratched at his chin. "That woman you mentioned... It's possible Altair has some of that ability. I'm sure I was hidden as I moved through the airport, yet he saw me right away when he bumped into me."

"It seems probable that Altair's bloodline holds a clue to that which Diwata has foretold." Bryndís's tone was pointed, and Magnús sighed.

"I understand. I'll stay close if I can and try to figure out what his heritage might be. Meanwhile, have you any idea what the 'Bishop's Shackles' or the 'Black Priest' could refer to?"

"I have been considering." Bryndís lifted the end of her braid to her lips and chewed on it as her eyes grew unfocused.

Magnús could feel his mother loosening from the present and slipping along the currents of her long life, many times his own four hundred years. Even without trying to speak mind-to-mind, he was aware of his mother's journey. The centuries yawned within her. They colored her aura in Time and Pain and Joy, swirls of light that had no name in the human tongue. Only another huldufólk would see the untold number of moments in the shimmer that surrounded his mother.

Magnús left quietly while Bryndís meditated so she wouldn't be distracted by his thoughts. As he waited in her library, he pulled out Karl's list of missing people and tried to identify a common thread among the disappearances. His oak chair, padded with a colorful cushion, rested next to the fireplace. The crackle of the fire kept drawing his attention away from his list, though. Instead of a pattern among the disappeared, his reverie turned to a young man with golden eyes. *An irritating, chattering human*, Magnús reminded himself.

Yet, despite the dire warning that loomed over their meeting at Keflavik, Magnús had been, well, slightly amused and touched by Altair's inexperience. No, by his *innocence*. For Altair, the world was still new. Even as he longed for a home, he drank in new experiences. Iceland wasn't his native land, but he could see beauty in it anyway, and he'd enjoyed Magnús's story.

It was so like Sigurjón, who had always treated each day as a gift. Most of Magnús's own people—jaded with the passage of time and the awareness they had years and decades and centuries to come still—never felt such a keen appreciation. They loved their rocks, their waterfalls, their volcanoes and glaciers, but with a patience that came from long familiarity.

No, it took a human to find joy in the mundane. Like Sigurjón. Like Altair.

Magnús felt a twinge of guilt he'd lied about the university hiring him as guide. With the strictures of the First Covenant, what else could he have done but lie? Posing as a driver and guide was the most subtle way he could think of to gather intelligence about the threat this Falcon might pose to Iceland and to track him to the Black Priest, whoever that was, without revealing the supernatural world to an outsider. The threat to the country had to be the primary consideration, and Magnús must be ready to do anything to fulfill his mission.

Stop. Altair is more than a mission. He is a human in deadly peril, exactly the vulnerable type I chose to protect.

The silver symbol engraved on one wall caught his attention. Curious to learn more about Altair—*professionally, just professionally*—he wondered if the sigil invoking Heimdallur Farsighted, the God Who Watched, could let him reach someone who wasn't a full huldufólk.

Magnús brushed his fingers along the etched lines that made up the glyph, whispering the brief incantation to Heimdallur. Bryndís's room faded from view as his mind soared into the darkness, a spirit seeking others of its kind. At first, he saw only the silver sigil, glowing to mark his tether to the material world and his body. The void quickly filled with stars, some near and others hundreds of miles away, each, one of the huldufólk. The nearest—and brightest—was Bryndís, though others of her household and of Hamarinn twinkled as well. That star in Reykjavik was Ólafur, and his friend Ingunn seemed to be in the northeast on her boat, sailing among a pod of dolphins...

Magnús resisted the pull of his kin and friends and instead called up a mental image of Altair. A spark appeared in the middle distance, paler than one that signified his kinfolk, yet warm and inviting. It drew him forward. He brushed against the spark, becoming aware only as he did so that Altair slept.

Through the tentative connection, Magnús sensed dreaming. He was briefly tempted to press further, to see what Altair dreamt about. Perhaps there would be a clue there. Yet invading dreams was not something the huldufólk did casually, either among their people or with humans. He knew stories of elves sending useful dreams to reward a human who had rendered a service, or horrific nightmares to punish one who offended. Magnús had never before considered reading or sending dreams to a human, even if the limitations of his mind-speech had made it possible. Given the threat, perhaps this one time he would be justified in looking...?

No. He firmly decided to end the experiment. Their time together in the car had convinced him Altair was the subject of Diwata's prophecy yet knew nothing about the strange things she mentioned. Magnús had no good reason to violate Altair's interior life further.

Still, he lingered for a moment in the half contact, reluctant to end it, as he enjoyed the unfamiliar terrain of a mostly human mind. It was a singular experience for Magnús, to brush against the texture of Altair's thoughts. Sigurjón had been fully human, and so Magnús had never been able to caress his lover in that way.

Altair, now. His mind felt rough, not yet worn smooth by the passage of dozens upon dozens of years. New, like an island formed of magma welling up from a tectonic split. And there was something else...

Magnús sharpened his focus. He sensed a place in Altair's mind that was akin to the core from which the huldufólk drew on their power of invisibility. Yet it was different, too. Winds blew there, and he could hear the faintest echo of beating wings. Energy pulsed in a rhythm entirely different than the quiet reserve of magic in each elf.

"—Begone, Meddler—"

A dark voice reverberated in Magnús's head, the menace in it unmistakable. An image of a fist encased in iron armor, black and somehow tasting like blood, appeared in the void and shoved against Magnús. He hurtled through darkness and away from Altair's sleeping mind, tumbling toward the sigil he'd invoked. The force of collision as his spirit hit his body threw him physically backward in the material world. He shouted as his skull cracked painfully on the stone floor of the library.

He was still moaning when Bryndís rushed into the room and went to her knees to cradle him.

"Magnús! What happened?"

"I...I don't know. Someone or something was hovering in the void around. It swatted me away. I came back to my body so swiftly that it threw me to the ground."

Cool magic from his mother's touch eased the headache quickly. She sank back on her heels. "The witch-child Diwata warned that sorcery is hiding Altair. Perhaps the voice you heard belongs to this Black Priest."

Magnús groaned. "If you're right, the Black Priest, or whoever that was, knows now that Altair was being regarded by one of us. That was a significant mistake on my part. I may have accelerated the danger with my actions."

Bryndís rose gracefully, then helped Magnús to his feet. One hand resting lightly on his shoulder, she said with determination, "I've asked Queen Hildur for an audience. It has occurred to me that if this Black Priest is going to bring armies we will need to raise our own."

Magnús snorted. "Hildur has always been quick to ignore human problems that don't directly threaten our folk. Why would she help?"

"*Queen* Hildur will help because the threat in Diwata's warning applies to the huldufólk as well as the humans. My heart tells me this voice you heard, this thing with power to break our speech, portends great danger for our people as well. Now I need to alert the queen."

"Mother, you don't seem worried about the part of the prophecy regarding me." Magnús feared he sounded petulant, but he was shaken by what the unseen presence had done to him. So much power...

Bryndís regarded him steadily, her head slightly tilted. "I am deeply concerned, Magnús. You are my only living child. We are immortal but not invulnerable, and your sisters were both killed in troubled times. I am also leader of this elf-town, and a royal advisor. This matter threatens all of our kind. I swear to you, though, if there is a way to avert the prophecy of your doom while still saving Iceland, I will take it."

Magnús knew he would get no more from her. He said, "When I see Altair later, I'll try to persuade him to leave Iceland. Maybe that would defeat the prophecy. If he won't leave…"

Until some other plan occurred to Magnús, he would have to accompany the Falcon constantly. Ignoring the troll investigation still felt wrong, but this affair with the Bishop's Shackles carried higher stakes, for his country as well as for himself.

He had just three days to unravel the mystery of Altair Fálkason, or one of them was fated to die.

CHAPTER

FOURTEEN

Altair jerked awake from his dream, heart thudding a mile a minute. He untangled himself wildly from the comforter, fumbled on the bedside lamp, and looked frantically around his small hotel room. Someone had been watching him; he was sure of it. His ears echoed with the sound of a voice shouting, very near. A dark, powerful voice that scared him.

But no one was there in the room with him. He could see the door from where he lay in bed, the latch in place.

Altair glanced nervously at the window with its blackout shades pulled down. Perhaps someone could have been trying to look in, despite the shades. Was that what he'd sensed in his sleep? No, his room was on the fourth floor, and he'd seen when he lowered the shades that there was no balcony or ledge out there.

Heart rate gradually slowing, Altair fell back against the mattress. It must have all been a dream—being watched, someone shouting...

Magnús!

That driver Magnús had been there, in his dream. Not in a

bad, creepy way; Magnús's presence had felt soothing, which was odd considering his cold manner in the car from the airport. Whatever had scared Altair awake, it wasn't Magnús.

Blinking his eyes into focus, he lifted his phone from the small bedside table where it was recharging. One-twenty in the afternoon, Iceland time, and it would be five hours earlier in Boston. His unease over the bad dream was fading, but he knew what he needed: a shower and then a call back home.

A faint smell of sulfur filled the bathroom when he turned on the shower. Altair had learned from his studies to expect that natural feature of Reykjavik's nearly unlimited hot water. After the shower, he stood dithering before the bathroom mirror before deciding he'd shave.

Whether from exhaustion or the lingering effects of his bad dream, Altair's hand shook slightly as he dragged a plastic razor over his throat. He jumped, yelping, when he nicked himself.

"Well, shit," he murmured, reaching for toilet paper to staunch the blood. By the time he looked in the mirror again, though, the blood had dried. He wet a fingertip and swiped his neck gently, but the cut he'd given himself was already gone.

Well, that was weird. Maybe the sulfurous water had a styptic effect? He'd have to look that up.

Shortly, layered in a tee-shirt, his warmest sweatshirt, and heavy pants, Altair propped up his phone to initiate a video call. Willa answered on the third ring.

Her image jerkily settled in as she leaned toward her phone. Jason entered the frame as well, lowering his face to look over Willa's shoulder.

"Hey, bud, how was the flight?" he asked

Altair told them about the trip, the drive from the airport with Magnús, and the plan to go explore Reykjavik.

"Don't forget why you're there," Willa said sternly. "Sightseeing is great and all, but you've got work to do."

"I won't forget," Altair assured her. How *could* he forget, when his home and job depended on it? But even with that pressure hanging over him, he felt fortified to face the frigid weather again.

"Have you checked on Missus Carmichael?" he asked Jason.

"Who? Oh, the lady downstairs. Don't worry, I'll stop by in a few days."

"I wish you were both here in Iceland with me," Altair remarked. "You'd really be amazed, I think."

Jason chuckled. "Aw, you'll see us sooner than you think." He glanced at Willa, who seemed to be glaring at him. "What? In two weeks, he'll be back in Boston."

Altair watched the byplay, slightly puzzled. He must be missing something.

Willa said, "I've got to get to class. Be careful of how you react to this driver person. Maybe Iceland isn't as accepting of gay people as Boston."

Altair grimaced at that. Willa could be right, and his ogling of Magnús might get him in trouble. Well, in any case, he'd somehow offended Magnús.

Resolving to keep a tighter leash on his reactions, he wiggled his fingers goodbye to Jason and Willa. He was reluctant to end the call, though, so he watched until Willa disconnected.

CHAPTER

FIFTEEN

At two o'clock, Altair blew on his hands outside his hotel. Although the sun shone down brilliantly, it was still damn cold compared to Boston at this time of year. Luckily, he'd brought his warmest jacket, figuring that when he got to one of the glaciers, he'd need it. He'd forgotten to pack gloves, though.

"Did you find something to eat?"

"Holy shit!" Altair whirled around at the brusque tone to find Magnús touching his shoulder. "Uh, sorry. I didn't see you there."

Magnús made no reply, but his eyes drifted to Altair's reddened hands. He muttered something sing-songy in Icelandic as he put his hands into the pocket of his own jacket, paused a moment, then pulled out a pair of blue mittens. Wordlessly, he offered them to Altair.

Altair flushed. No doubt Magnús was mocking the silly American who was unprepared for a country that actually had *Ice* in its name.

"That's okay," he muttered. "I'll be fine when we walk. Just need to get the blood pumping, right?"

Magnús stared levelly at him and said nothing, nor did he withdraw the mittens. After a moment, his eyes softened from what Altair took as judgment to something that might have been concern. Or kindness.

Reluctantly, Altair took the offering. "Thank you," he said to the pavement as he tugged on a mitten. "I'm the idiot who didn't think to check the weather forecast, or to pack gloves. It's warming up back home, so I forgot I probably would need heavier gear for Iceland."

"It's not a problem," Magnús said, his voice sounding less unfriendly than when they parted. "The weather here...well, let's call it unpredictable." He cocked his head at Altair, though. "Do you really want to carry that all day?"

Altair blinked in surprise as he discovered his black satchel was slung over his shoulder. He had no memory of picking it up before he left the room. "Wow, I must be still half-asleep."

"Do you want to take it back to your room before we go?"

"No!" Altair was startled at the vehemence that came out of his mouth. "Um, sorry. No, it's fine. I might...need it."

Magnús seemed about to speak, but his attention suddenly went to the side of the hotel building.

"Hey, these are really warm." Altair held up his hands, flexing wool-covered fingers like sock puppets. It was almost like the things contained hand warmers, he was so toasty. And they fit perfectly, which seemed odd given that Magnús's hands were bigger than Altair's.

Magnús didn't comment. He'd moved closer to the wall, peering intently at some graffiti painted there, about waist high.

Altair couldn't see anything special about the tag. It was a shape, in thick red lines that reminded him of one of the tiles Willa sometimes used when she was fortune-telling at a party.

"Where have I seen that before?" Magnús muttered.

Altair leaned in as well, intrigued now. "Is it a gang sign? Um, are there even gangs in Iceland?"

"It's a rune," Magnús answered in a distracted tone, still focused on the graffiti. "Gangs aren't really an issue here. Some want-to-be Hells Angels have been a problem from time to time. A few incidents recently that officials call organized crime. But I've not heard of a gang here like those you have in America. Still, perhaps Karl knows…?" He stretched out his hand to the painted symbol but jerked back quickly as if it were hot.

"Uh, Karl? Is that, like, your boss?" Altair asked.

Magnús rubbed his thumb and fingers together, frowning at them. "Hm? Oh. No, Karl is my friend. He works with the Search and Rescue teams. They get called when someone falls down an ice crevasse or is caught in an avalanche, for example."

"That sounds heroic. And dangerous."

Magnús straightened up and turned away from the wall. "It can be, I suppose. But Karl is highly trained."

Now, why did Altair feel a pang of jealousy at that? *I'm being so stupid.* Aloud, he suggested, "Why don't you take a picture and send it to him?"

Magnús shrugged. "I don't use a smartphone. But I'll sketch it out and drop it off at his house later." He scanned Altair up and down, all business again. "Now, do you need any other protective gear?"

Distracted by the strangeness of Magnús not using a smartphone, Altair stammered, "Um, hopefully not. I do have a scarf and another sweater in my suitcase back in my hotel room. These hiking boots are waterproof. Or maybe water-resistant? I forget."

Magnús glanced down at his feet, and Altair resisted the urge to tuck the more scuffed boot behind his ankle. He'd debated a new pair before this trip, but funds were just too low.

Without further comment, Magnús started walking, and Altair

followed. Playing tour guide, at least, seemed to make Magnús unclench. He clearly loved his city and his country. As they passed along the waterfront, Magnús pointed out a large, silvery sculpture that looked like a giant scorpion skeleton ("It's called Sólfar and represents a dream boat as an ode to sun and light") and a large building of green glass ("That's Harpa, the concert hall. At night, the panels light up in a show that pays tribute to the aurora").

Altair soon found himself looking at the landscape and buildings with appreciation. Plus, Magnús began to pepper Altair with questions about his trip, his plans, even his family. Altair had no idea why Magnús found his project and his life interesting, but the attention was flattering.

"Professor Milton is the one who persuaded me to apply for the grant to come here. I'm his teaching assistant. I didn't see the connection between Iceland and my dissertation at first. I definitely didn't think I'd have a shot at a grant."

"You speak warmly of this professor."

"He's been great to me. I mean really great," Altair said. "I was lucky enough to get into one of his classes when I started graduate school. I was lost at first. No one I met in foster care had even been to college or planned to go, so my undergrad work was challenging enough. Professor Milton could tell I was nervous; he invited me specially to come to his office hours. He made me realize I belonged there and could really do the work. Willa was also in one of his classes—"

"Willa?"

"My roommate. She's, like, the sister I always wanted. She let me move into the spare room in her place, lowered the rent to what I could afford. Willa and Professor Milton pushed me to work hard and really invested a lot of time in my studies. They're still on me, to finish my doctorate. Everything I have I owe to them."

Magnús looked puzzled. "You're a college graduate, in

advanced studies. You earned a grant to travel internationally. You must have had something to do with your own success."

"Oh, well, if you put it that way... I mean, sure, I worked hard. But I don't know if I could have made it in grad school without them. Or Jason, that's Willa's boyfriend." Watching the ragged toe of his hiking boot, Altair confessed in a low voice, "I sorta think of him as my brother."

"You mentioned the foster care system," Magnús said, sounding cautious. "Do they not have counselors or advisors in the United States who could help you in college? Or foster parents who are college educated?"

Altair snorted. "My last foster dad just wanted the check for taking in as many of us as he could cram into three bedrooms. The older kids were unpaid babysitters for the younger ones. I don't think the guy finished high school, let alone college, so he was no help. I mean, there were good people in Child Services. They were just so busy that it wasn't like they could take the time to guide one goofball kid who was nutty about energy systems."

"I'm sorry you went through that," Magnús said somberly.

Altair shrugged and looked away. "It wasn't that bad. Really. Just..." He swallowed hard but made himself say it. "Professor Milton and Willa and Jason. They were, like, the first people to take an interest, I guess. Everyone always left, my whole life. Or sent me away. But not them. They're family to me."

"If it isn't too personal, may I ask why you don't return to Boston right away?" Magnús asked, a bit awkwardly. "You aren't really prepared for the weather, and I sense that you aren't enthusiastic to be here." He held up a hand before Altair could protest. "I don't mean any offense. I merely wonder whether this is the best place for you."

Altair sighed. Yeah, he could just picture himself arriving back in Boston, calling Jason for a ride from the airport. The judgmental look Willa would give him when he walked through the door, the frustration he would find from Professor Milton, the disappointment from Uncle Trausti. How long would it be before they told him to find a new living situation, a new career path...? No. It simply wasn't possible to go.

Jaw clenched, Altair muttered, "I *have* to see this through, or I might lose everything I've been working for."

"Ah." Thankfully, Magnús dropped the subject after one more long stare into Altair's eyes. By now, Altair was used to that tickle in his head, so he didn't even swat at it.

Though it was interesting he only felt that tickle when Magnús was around. He suddenly flashed to the strange dream from earlier. He'd woken in alarm, and somehow Magnús had been tied up in it—

Magnús started walking in the direction of the water and the mountain beyond that Altair had noticed before. "Is there anything else in particular you want to see in Reykjavik?" he asked.

Altair pushed aside his odd thoughts. He was in a strange land with a handsome man willing to play tour guide. No wonder his dreams were confounding. Falling in step, his legs worked to keep up with Magnús's long stride. "The church we saw, uh, Hall-grimsh—"

"Hallgrímskirkja."

"Yeah, that one. That looks pretty dope. I'm meeting my grant advisor tomorrow at the School of Energy in the University of Reykjavik, and she's going to take me through the HFC Nordic plant. Do you know any museums with exhibits about Iceland's power systems?"

"I could probably get us into one. Anything else?"

Altair suddenly recalled Jason's remark from just before they'd left the apartment, and his cheeks burned. "Um, no. That's it."

"What are you thinking of?" Magnús sounded curious, not brusque.

"It's nothing. Just something my roommate mentioned."

He risked a peek up and was surprised to catch a grin forming on Magnús's lips. It was a good look on that normally shuttered face.

"Are you talking about the Phallological Museum?"

Oh god, Altair's face was warmer than his fingers in borrowed mittens. "Jason said... I mean, we don't have to—"

"No, it's fine. We can definitely go to the penis museum."

"You mean it's real?"

"Oh yes, and very popular with tourists." Magnús gave him a wink. "Icelanders are fascinated by penises, too. Seals, polar bears, foxes, squirrels. Of course, the whale specimens might make you feel, um..."

"Inadequate?" Altair chuckled.

"Or jealous."

After a joke like that, Magnús seemed much more human. Altair found it increasingly easy to relax around him. He had a twinge of guilt that he wasn't back in his hotel room, working on his thesis or studying his notes like Willa would have wanted. But understanding the way a city like Reykjavik utilized electricity and hot water generated by geothermal energy seemed like a valid use of his time, too.

The more they walked, the more Altair could start to see the harmony of design, the love of nature, that guided Icelandic art and architecture. Many buildings they passed had huge, colorful murals painted on them, in a variety of styles and themes. One in particular arrested Altair's attention. Halting, they stood side by side as they studied the artwork.

On a black background filled with stars and swirling nebulae, an enormous tree spread roots and branches. Each branch seemed to end in a round shape, almost like fruit hanging on the tree. In all, Altair counted nine globes, painted in unique styles. One was golden and wreathed in a rainbow, another pair suggested ice and fire, yet another seemed desolate and gray.

"This is awesome," Altair said. "I have no idea what it means, but I love it."

"The ash tree represents Yggdrasill. The World Tree," Magnús offered. "The gods formed the cosmos from the body of the frost giant Ýmir. They fashioned nine worlds, connected by Yggdrasill. The golden one painted there is Ásgarður, home of the Æsir, the Norse gods you've probably heard of like Óðinn and Þór. Vanaheimur holds another divine race, the Vanir. Frost giants live in Jötunheimar, fire giants in Muspellsheimur. Niflheimur is for the dead. Dwarves reside in Niðavellir.

"These"—Magnús pointed at two globes, one painted as if glowing with internal light, the other in soul-sucking darkness—"represent Álfheimur and Svartálfaheimur, where the light elves and the dark elves come from. And this, of course"—he pointed at a green-and-blue orb—"is Earth, which we call Miðgarður."

"We?"

"Excuse me?"

"You said 'we' call it, uh, Mitt-garter? Oh, like Midgard! Anyway, do you mean Icelanders?"

A rosy tinge grew on Magnús's alabaster skin, which Altair found unfair. The man was so handsome already that he shouldn't be allowed to blush beautifully as well.

"Yes, Icelanders," Magnús finally said, then added quickly, "Let's visit Hallgrímskirkja."

That's yet another change of subject. There was something Magnús was hiding.

It wasn't in Altair's nature to be so trusting normally. His reaction to Magnús was curious, especially given how abrupt the guy could be. Altair knew he should be warier, but he had to admit to himself that he continued to feel safe. It wasn't as simple as Magnús's looks. There was a, a...*presence* to the man. Strength, a connection to the light.

Deciding to trust his instincts, Altair let another mystery go. For now.

They walked away from the mural and, according to Magnús, headed toward a sculpture garden near the center of the city that was on the way to the church. After a block or two, Magnús murmured, "If you don't mind me asking, what happened to your parents?"

Altair sighed. "My dad left us when I was three. I don't really remember him, only that he used to take me everywhere with him. And that he smelled like a pine forest. But one day he was just... gone. The airline he worked for said he quit one day and took off, no forwarding address."

"And your mother?" Magnús asked gently, bringing Altair out of his reverie.

"Car crash when I was ten. We had no other family I knew of. My mom told me once her own parents died in Bahrain before I was born, and she didn't think my dad had any other relatives. So, CPS sent me to an orphanage for a while. Then to a bunch of foster families."

"I can see why your professor and friends are so important to you."

Altair glanced up at Magnús, touched by the sympathy in his voice. "Yeah, so..." He sighed. "I wish we'd known about Trausti while my mom was still alive. That might have made things better, because she always had to work so hard to keep a roof over our heads."

"Trausti?"

"My uncle. My dad's brother, only we never knew he'd even had a brother. Two years ago, he found me at the college I went to. He said that Dad came and lived with him in California for a while but never once mentioned that he had a family somewhere. Then Dad married some other woman and had a kid with her."

"That's...awful." Magnús sounded sad for him.

Altair shrugged. "It wasn't until Dad died of a heart attack, apparently, that Trausti learned he'd abandoned us. Trausti tried to make it up to me, even though there was no way he could have known I was out there in foster care."

"That's interesting," Magnús said. "Your mother was of Arabic origin, I take it? But Trausti sounds Nordic."

"That's right. My Dad was from Iceland, or at least his parents were."

"Do you know anything else about your heritage?" Magnús's sympathetic tone had changed. He suddenly sounded eager, almost insistent.

"Very little," Altair admitted, a bit cautiously. "Well, actually, Trausti mentioned his mother was from a town called, um, Akureyri. Am I saying that right? He knew I'd won this grant—"

"Earned," Magnús interjected.

"Okay, earned this grant to come to Iceland. He told me about how his mother moved to the States, but used to talk about growing up here. She told him stories about volcanos that erupted with short notice, hard times for the fishing industry, history. Stuff like that."

Sensing that Magnús had stopped walking, Altair stopped too. He looked up at the tall man, whose eyes had narrowed in puzzlement.

"Your grandmother is from Iceland, your long-lost uncle has stories about Iceland, and you earned a grant to study in Iceland. Isn't that all a bit...coincidental?"

A buzzing rose in Altair's ears for a moment. He looked up at the sky. Perhaps a plane was flying overhead? The last few minutes seemed to blur and fade away.

"Altair?"

The buzzing was so loud. Was the plane coming in for a landing and that's why it sounded shrill and close? He swayed...

"Altair."

"Hm? Oh, sorry. I lost the plot there for a moment, I guess. Must be the jet lag. Hey, what were we talking about? Oh, my sister. I mean Willa. Yeah, she's been amazing to me. Didn't even blink when I came out to her as gay."

Magnús just stared, brows furrowed. Silence seemed to stretch between them, and a questioning look had crept into Magnús's face.

Suddenly Altair heard what he'd said aloud. He gulped as Willa's warning crept back into his head: *Maybe Iceland isn't as accepting of gay people as Boston.* Was he about to find out the bad way from six-foot-whatever Magnús about intolerance?

The hard, quizzical look in Magnús's eyes faded. Gently, he said, "Gay. Straight. Anything in between. I've always found that love is love, and those who have a problem with another's orientation are jealous."

Altair felt his shoulders unclench. "Yeah?"

"Yes. Though now I understand better why you want to see the penis museum." Magnús added with a wink.

"Shut up," Altair laughed, pushing at him. "It's scientific curiosity, that's all."

CHAPTER

SIXTEEN

Later, as they walked past coffee shops, restaurants, and tourist shops full of Viking-themed kitsch, Altair peeked again into the bag he carried. The coffee mug from the Phallological Museum's gift shop rustled in its tissue paper wrapping.

"You didn't have to get this for me," he muttered, though he was beyond touched that Magnús had bought him a present.

Magnús didn't meet Altair's eye but just looked at the sidewalk as he muttered, "Surely a student needs something to drink his coffee from."

"Oh, I do. But if I leave a mug with a dick for a handle in the staff room back home, it might get Professor Lowell worked up. She's got to be eighty, and she shows up for her classes in a sweater and pearls every day."

"I was going to buy you an Icelander's favorite snack next. Now I'm not sure you'd appreciate it." Magnús raised an eyebrow at him, but Altair felt pretty sure he was being teased, not judged.

"Food? Yes, please. This hike has me starving."

"All right then, but I need you to keep in mind what a serious culinary experience I'm about to share with you."

The light edge to Magnús's words made Altair feel a bit shimmery inside. Five minutes later, standing in a long line for a takeaway window, he giggled up at Magnús.

"Seriously? A hot dog?"

"Not just a hot dog, you American tourist. It's an Icelandic delicacy. This place"—Magnús gestured at the tiny shack amid lots of construction—"it's been around for decades. The hot dogs contain lamb. The hu—*we* eat them with fried and raw onions, a little sauce, and ketchup made from apples."

"Apples? You're kidding."

Magnús raised his hand in an oath. "You'll never taste American ketchup again without thinking how superior ours is."

The line moved quickly, and soon Magnús was speaking in Icelandic to the girl at the window. A few minutes later, she passed over two hot dogs in buns, each wrapped in paper, and two bottles of water.

Magnús led them to a nearby bench. Once seated, he handed Altair a paper-wrapped package with great solemnity. "Be honored, Altair Fálkason. You are about to partake in an Icelandic tradition."

Fighting a grin, Altair bowed his head. "Thank you, oh guru of all things Scandinavian, for educating this ignorant tourist."

Magnús sighed. "Iceland is not part of Scandinavia. Say that in the wrong crowd and you might incite an argument."

As Altair pondered that, he unwrapped one end of the parcel and looked at his hot dog dubiously. The shape was familiar, the aroma had him salivating, but the condiments looked a little alarming. "Apple ketchup, huh? Okay, here goes." He took a bite, teeth breaking through the crisp casing, the tender meat, and soft bun. Fried and raw onions combined with the sweetness of the ketchup to make the flavor of the lamb pop.

"Oh shit, that's really good," he mumbled around a mouthful.

Magnús watched intently as Altair took a second bite, blue eyes fixed on Altair's fingers as he brought them to his mouth to lick off some sauce.

"My son, what a nice surprise."

Altair whipped his head up and around to find the owner of the lilting, alto voice. A tall woman stood just behind their bench, her pale hand resting on Magnús's shoulder. Their facial features were quite similar, though this woman's hair was honey-gold to Magnús's silver-blond, and her eyes a deeper blue. She wore an elegant green suit that looked, to Altair's admittedly untrained eye, slightly old-fashioned and really expensive.

But her face! Unlined, serene, looking devoid of makeup yet regal... No way this woman was old enough to be Magnús's mother.

Magnús rose and turned to kiss the woman's cheek formally. "Bryndís, you look well. Thank you for our last meeting. May I present my friend, Altair Fálkason?"

Altair got to his feet, still clutching his half-eaten hot dog. He didn't know what to do with it, or whether his fingers were all sticky.

Bryndís smiled gently as she took the fingers of his hand not encumbered by a hot dog and clasped them. "It's lovely to meet you, Altair." Her eyes stayed fixed on his, and she didn't let go of his hand.

As the elegant woman gazed at him, Altair distinctly heard the trickle of a brook, and smelled pine trees warmed by the summer sun. Not just a few random trees in a park, though. This was an ancient forest, spread across a mountain, filling a vale where no human had yet set foot...

"Altair? My mother asked where you are from?" Magnús's voice startled Altair, making him shake his head to alertness.

"I'm so sorry! My mind wandered for a moment. Still jet lag, I guess." He added lamely, "I'm, uh, I'm from Boston. In the States."

Bryndís smiled at him. "I know where Boston is, though I've never been. I'm sure it's lovely." Finally, she released his fingers, and the noises of a busy city again filled his ears. "I don't want to interrupt your lunch. Please, sit."

She gestured at the bench as if inviting Altair and Magnús into her parlor. Into her throne room? Actually, that fit better. Magnús took a seat again, with Bryndís to his right as Altair sank back down on his left.

"Altair is an interesting name," Bryndís was saying. "Is there a story behind it?"

An image of Altair's mother popped into his head suddenly. The vision was incredibly clear, maybe clearer than he'd pictured her in years. Weird. It was like the image was pulled from his memories.

"Uh, the name is Arabic, actually," he stammered. "My mother's family was from Bahrain originally, but she grew up in Massachusetts. That's where she met my dad."

Bryndís closed her eyes and cocked her head as if listening. "Falcon," she murmured. Then, opening her eyes and looking at Magnús, she said, "Altair means falcon."

Altair nodded self-consciously. "My father was a pilot. I suppose that's why they chose the name."

"And your father was descended from Icelanders, you said," Magnús commented softly.

Altair shrugged. "Well, my grandmother was from Iceland, at least. I'm not sure about my dad's father."

"Do you remember her? Your grandmother?" Bryndís asked, watching Altair like he was fascinating. Like he was someone significant, instead of an underdressed graduate student with a half-eaten hot dog in his hand.

"No, I never met her. Actually, I didn't know anything about her until recently. It's kind of complicated."

Magnús and Bryndís shared a look that lasted a beat. Altair squinted one eye. He could almost hear words in the silence between them. Something like...not eggy hulled you folk.

Bryndís looked at him sharply then. Flustered, Altair took another bite of his hot dog.

"Magnús, my son," Bryndís said thoughtfully. "Have you taken Altair to one of our swimming pools yet? Sundhöllin is quite near." To Altair, she smiled and said, "It's a unique experience. Icelanders use public swimming pools the way the Romans used agoras, as a place to meet and catch up on news and gossip."

"I've read about those," Altair said excitedly. "Geothermal pools, right? There's so much energy here in Iceland, just waiting to be tapped."

Magnús shared a small grin with Bryndís. "Altair is an engineering student, you see, here to understand our power sources."

"And we have so many," Bryndís replied, the edges of her lips just tilting into a smile. "Not all of them are understood, even now. Well"—she rose gracefully—"I must be going. I have an appointment with Hildur to discuss matters."

That cryptic comment was delivered to Magnús, who just nodded at her. Altair wondered what Bryndís did. Perhaps a government official of some kind?

He watched the elegant woman leave, gliding away. She stepped out of sight behind a truck for a moment but then didn't reappear. How odd.

"Have you finished your hot dog?" Magnús asked, sounding almost eager. "If so, I think Bryndís was right. We should spend an hour at Sundhöllin. The water will be wonderfully soothing after your long flight."

Stuffing the rest of his hot dog into his mouth, putting

notions about Bryndís out of his mind, Altair mumbled around it, "Lead on. I'm game for anything."

CHAPTER

SEVENTEEN

Altair was *not* game for this.

He looked around the changing room of the public swimming pool where Magnús had brought him. From somewhere, Magnús had acquired swimsuits for both of them. Already, he was stripping off his sweater and pants.

Altair swallowed nervously. What had he been thinking, to agree to this? He didn't like being in the water, and most especially he didn't like the idea of taking off his clothes in front of a handsome Viking. His slender physique would look weak and childlike next to Magnús. Plus, there was a definite risk of embarrassing himself with an awkward hard-on.

He kept his face turned toward the wall of painted, wooden lockers so he wouldn't get caught ogling Magnús's amazing body. Even from the corner of his eye, though, he could see long, lean muscles covered in alabaster skin. So. Much. *Skin.* He stripped awkwardly, stuffed his clothes in a locker along with his satchel and his gift mug from Magnús, and fumbled behind on the bench for his bathing suit.

"Oh, don't bother with that yet," Magnús said. "We have to shower first. Come along."

"Shower?" Altair squeaked, surprised enough that he glanced around at Magnús.

Oh god, he was looking at Magnús. *All* of Magnús.

Look up, look up, he yelled at himself.

"Yes, shower." Magnús gestured impatiently for Altair to follow him. "Everyone showers naked here, with soap, before getting into the pools. Do you not do that in America?"

Sure enough, as Altair glanced timidly around the locker room, several men and boys were heading to the shower area, towels and suits over an arm or loosely held. No one seemed fussed or uncomfortable being stark naked.

Suck it up, he ordered as he hurried after Magnús. *No one's looking, no one cares that you're nude. Just fit in.*

Easy for you to say, he answered himself. *Look at these guys. Tall, fit—everything I'm not.*

"You look fine," Magnús said quietly over his shoulder. "We're all so used to going naked that we don't think twice about one more bare bum. Come on, quick shower and then it's over."

Altair nodded, only realizing as he draped his suit on a hook outside the communal shower how peculiar it was that Magnús had read his worries so precisely. Now that he thought about it, that had been happening a lot all day. He risked a peek to where Magnús lathered himself, two shower heads down. What exactly was going on here?

The renewed questions about Magnús took his mind off the awkwardness of being naked in a roomful of strangers. Following Magnús's lead, he pulled on his swimsuit, stuffed his towel in a rack with dozens of others, and left the locker room for the outdoor pool area.

Open to the sky, the coping around the huge, rectangular pool was concrete and terrazzo. A series of diving platforms at one end, and aluminum ladders spaced around for access, looked similar to pools Altair had visited in the States.

What amazed him, though, was the water itself. Despite the chilly spring air, the facility was warm and humid. A blanket of steam drifted lazily above the water, through which he could see pale blue tiles with darker blue used to denote lanes. Instead of the chlorine smell he expected, the air was mineral and slightly salty.

The pool was filled with ten or so people, swimming laps. Parallel to the pool and nearly as long was a hot tub of sorts, jets bubbling away while even more people sat in pairs or groups, chatting. A third outdoor pool, quite shallow, contained children playing in a small fountain and teenagers lounging casually as they talked and laughed. The atmosphere was relaxed and festive.

Magnús looked back and forth as if deciding. "Cold plunge over there. The dry sauna and the hot pots are up those stairs," he said, pointing.

"Hot pots?" Altair asked.

"Uh, what is the term in English... Hot baths?"

"Hot tubs."

"Yes, that's it. Hot tubs with a range of temperatures."

"This is so cool," Altair muttered, eyes darting around. The engineer in him tried to figure out where the intake pipes were to bring the naturally heated water to the pool and hot tub. "How do they deal with wastewater? Is it recycled, or is there a purification plant on premises?"

Magnús chuckled. "I'm afraid it's all magic to me. I couldn't tell you how they built the place, only that it works."

"Sorry, I get carried away. Maybe they'll be able to tell me at the university tomorrow. Um, what do you want to do first?"

Magnús looked around speculatively, between darting glances back at Altair. It was beginning to make Altair uncomfortable. After several moments, Magnús said, "There's no one in the plunge pool. Let's start there to get the blood invigorated. Then we'll enjoy the warm water more."

Altair followed, surprised at Magnús's fast pace. As they hurried toward the plunge pool, two small children pattered that way as well, a tired-looking man following behind. Altair barely caught a curious twitch in Magnús's fingers, like he was drawing a symbol in the air. The children altered direction without even slowing, then jumped into the indoor lap pool.

Altair blinked to clear his vision. Maybe it was a trace of steam, but he could have sworn that something shiny hung in the air where Magnús had just made his gesture. He stopped for a closer look, but whatever the illusion had been, it was gone now.

Magnús stood by the edge of the small plunge pool, his body positioned as if to block Altair from others in the facility. The look on his face was curiously intent as he gestured to the water.

"Please, you first. Remember it will be a little cold, but the shock is good for the system."

Altair shivered, both at the thought of the icy water and at Magnús's intensity. He moved reluctantly to the steps that led down into the pool. Magnús leaned forward a little, eyes glinting.

"Here goes," Altair mumbled, then stepped quickly down into the water. "Oh crap!" he exclaimed, too loudly. "It's freezing!" He jumped up and down in the pool, rubbing his arms. "How long do I have to stay in here?"

The eager look on Magnús's face melted away. Now it was... disappointed?

"Hm? Oh, not long. In fact, that's probably enough."

Magnús looked away, and Altair felt himself deflate.

CHAPTER

EIGHTEEN

Bryndís's guess was wrong, Magnús thought. *So where does that leave us?*

Barely paying attention, he gnawed on his lower lip as he led Altair back to the outdoor hot tub. They followed the tiled steps down into the warm water, surrounded by mist that rose from its surface. He sat on an underwater bench, powerful jets churning the water around them.

Bryndís hadn't been able to identify a trace of elven blood. Continuing the conversation they'd begun mind-to-mind, she'd thought to Magnús that Altair might be descended from a nykur instead.

«Many of the water-wights followed the Vikings on their raids, and a fair few never returned. One or two might have gone to North America with the humans and created hybrid offspring there.»

«Is there a reliable test?» Magnús had asked.

«Not one I could avow. If Altair is part nykur, perhaps sudden contact with Icelandic water might trigger a transformation.»

And that was why she'd suggested the public swimming pool,

of course. But now the experiment had failed, and Magnús's heart was heavy.

Not an elf, not a water spirit. So what *was* Altair? What else could account for the magic in him? Half-trolls were not unheard of, though pretty rare. Magnús shuddered. What kind of human would mate with one of those foul, murdering things?

The prophecy had spoken of a falcon, which indicated a spirit of the air. But he couldn't think of any. Other than Gammur, the great guardian Eagle, of course, but Gammur was unable to leave Iceland's shores. The land wight couldn't have gone to America to sire a child.

The Nornir were seriously out of their minds to involve Magnús. If Altair refused to leave Iceland—and Magnús had felt Altair's commitment to staying—then the only other step he could think to take was bringing Altair to Hamarinn. Perhaps Óli or the witch would be able to learn more.

"Did I, uh, do something wrong?" Altair asked uncertainly from where he sat in the warm water close by.

Magnús spun his head around, blinking at the misery in Altair's voice. He suddenly realized how long he'd been withdrawn into his own speculations, ignoring the very person he was supposed to protect. Now Altair clung to one of the ladders, looking dejected.

Guilt soured the hot dog in Magnús's gut. Here he was, treating Altair as a puzzle to be solved and not as a human. A human who, unbeknownst to him, had a death sentence hanging over his head if Magnús should fail in his task.

"I'm sorry, I was distracted there for a moment. No, of course you haven't done anything wrong."

A look of cautious relief appeared on Altair's face. "I'm taking up so much of your time. Maybe you weren't hired to spend all afternoon with me."

Ah yes, his little lie, to ease his task. But what was his task? Just to keep Altair alive? Follow him to the Black Priest? First, though, he could course-adjust with an equally small truth.

"I'm not being paid to swim with you. I brought you because I thought you'd enjoy it."

A small, shy grin appeared on Altair's generous lips and spread a bit. Magnús experienced a curious warmth at Altair's smile. He was quite handsome, in a way that struck Magnús as exotic, with his bronzed skin, easy grin, and near-golden eyes.

"Really? Um, I'm liking it a lot. So, uh, thank you."

"You're welcome."

A few minutes later, they moved on to the indoor pool, which was largely empty, so they could just splash around in the warm water a bit. Altair clearly enjoyed the pool, even if he wasn't a water spirit. A few people passed by in steady rhythms, swimming their laps up and back. The cavernous room echoed with the gentle splash of their strokes.

As they drifted in the water out of the way of serious swimmers, Magnús sent out his thoughts, hoping to reach Ólafur and ask about a meeting. He couldn't find his cousin's mind at this distance, though, not without a sigil to help him. Until he could reach Óli and Diwata, it seemed his best option continued to be staying near to Altair.

Casually, Magnús asked, "So, what's your itinerary after today?"

"Let's see." Altair tipped his head back, squinting at a skylight through the steam drifting upward. "Tomorrow I'm still here in Reykjavik, at the University. Two plant visits scheduled, I believe. The next morning I'm catching a flight to, um, Egilsstaðir. Did I say that right?"

"Close enough," Magnús said, suppressing a grin. It shouldn't be so endearing to hear Altair murder the Icelandic language.

"There's a big plant there I'm to study. I'll be in that area for two days because there's so much to see. The dam, the power station, oh, and there's an aluminum plant that gets most of its power from, uh—"

"Fljótsdalur Power Station," Magnús offered, seeing the name in Altair's mind.

Thus engaged about his studies, Altair was wide open, even to Magnús's limited gift. Random thoughts about studies and about making the people back in Boston proud—Willa, Jason, Professor Milton, this found family of his—darted across his brain. So tempting to press a little further, to see what Altair might not even realize he knew about the Black Priest...

"—We warned you before, you stupid interloper—"

The dark voice shouting in Magnús's head was his only warning. Water around his legs tugged harshly, then swirled. In moments it churned and frothed. Altair yelped and hugged the aluminum ladder to keep from getting pulled in.

Bands of water tightened around Magnús's chest and legs. He was sucked straight down to the bottom of the pool. The water spun him round and round, disorienting him so badly he couldn't tell which way was air. He'd had no chance to prepare a breath, and quickly he ached with the need for oxygen. His toes scraped painfully against the side of the pool as he was tossed like a rag doll, then his head collided with the metal stair. He tried to sketch a glyph, but he couldn't speak the words of a spell underwater. Clawing at any surface, smooth tile skittered by under his fingers. Air. He needed air—

A hand gripped his hair and pulled, but the current was so harsh he thought his scalp might be torn free. Lungs burning, he reached up to swat away at the new torment. A second hand gripped his flailing wrist, and suddenly he felt himself being pulled. His head broke the surface as Altair tugged him free of the whirlpool.

"Aaaaaah," he gasped, filling his lungs with precious breath.

Face pale, eyes wide, Altair stammered, "A-are you all right?"

Magnús looked wildly around him, expecting to be sucked under again at any moment, but the water was calming. Except for Altair and himself, the pool had emptied; however, shouting or crying humans crowded the coping around it. Apparently, they'd all been able to get out when the eddy, or whirlpool, or whatever it was began.

Everyone but Magnús and Altair. Who could have died because Magnús hadn't been able to react fast enough to the attack.

Heart pounding, he managed to nod. "I'm fine." Shoving aside self-recriminations, he realized they'd better leave the area before people asked too many questions. "Come on. I think it's time to go."

Altair followed him out of the pool and toward the locker room, anxiety radiating off him in waves. One of the women who'd been in the pool pointed at them and shouted something. Whether it was concern for his safety or a complaint he'd caused the phenomenon, Magnús couldn't hear. He needed a minute to process what had almost happened. Alone, he would have made himself invisible, but he couldn't wrap Altair in light the same way.

Or could he? He'd never actually tried to shield anyone; other elves would protect themselves, and he was usually hiding *from* humans, not taking one with him.

He put an arm around Altair's shoulder, leaning on him slightly as if he needed the support. Which wasn't entirely untrue. That sorcerous attack—it couldn't be anything else—had shaken him.

He pulled enough magic to weave the light. It was sloppily done because at least a few people had already been looking at the two men from the center of the maelstrom. A small cry went up as they vanished. He had to hope that in the steam and the general pandemonium, the detail would be missed and that he hadn't violated the First Covenant.

He tugged Altair to the locker room, mercifully empty as people had rushed to see what the commotion was about. Quickly he dropped his suit, swiped a fast towel over his skin and hair, then pulled on his clothes. Altair must have caught his intensity because he didn't ask questions but mirrored Magnús. In only two minutes, they were slipping outside to the street.

Altair cooperated, moving as quickly as Magnús urged, until they were a block away from Sundhöllin. As they rounded a corner onto a quiet side street, Altair unexpectedly jerked to a stop. Magnús turned back to look down at him.

"What. The hell. Was *that*?" Altair demanded, eyes flashing.

"I think, uh, the geothermal system must have had a problem." Magnús looked up and down the street, then inspiration hit. "There's been some recent volcanic activity. The Reykjanes volcano, it began erupting a month ago. All that lava flow must have produced unusual heat in the water that feeds—"

"Nice try," Altair said witheringly, "but that's not how science actually works. One minute you were squinting at me like you always do, then I heard a voice, and then you were drowning. In a whirlpool. Inside a public swimming pool."

"Did you hit your head?" Magnús tried. "I got banged up and barely remember what happened. Maybe you did too."

"How do you say 'bullshit' in Icelandic?"

"Kjaftæði," Magnús muttered.

"Then that."

Tiny, fierce, face ruddier than normal, fists on hips as he glared up at Magnús with eyes on fire—Altair was rightly calling him out on his lies. Dammit.

The First Covenant didn't consider a situation like this. Altair was technically an outsider, and so Magnús could be punished for revealing too much. On the other hand, Altair had a clear connection to the land, he was named in a prophecy about the fate of the entire country, and he had been subjected to sorcery within Iceland. Surely those factors would be enough to defend Magnús's actions.

He was going to take the risk. Altair had no idea what he was up against, and his chances of survival were better if he knew more.

Magnús sighed. "What do you know about elves?"

CHAPTER

NINETEEN

Magnús winced as Altair scoffed. "Elves. Right. Are you going to try to tell me that phenomenon at the pool was caused by little elves? Ky-aff... oh, forget it. I just call bullshit again."

Altair sounded suspicious, but the confusion Magnús could sense was also tinged with hurt. He could read in Altair's surface thoughts that Altair believed Magnús was toying with him, or about to lie.

To be fair, Magnús had already tried that and would do so again if he thought it would work and keep Altair safe. His luck didn't tend that way, though.

Magnús glanced around desperately. He was not equipped to explain the world of the elves and spirits of Iceland to a young man from America who didn't speak a word of Icelandic and had not been raised on their folklore. Karl, for example, had grown up with a witch for a father and never questioned what Magnús was, back when Magnús rescued him from an avalanche.

That was a thought—could he get Karl here to explain? Anyone would be better at this than Magnús.

No, there wasn't time to call Karl, and besides, he might be caught up in the troll business. Magnús had to decide quickly where and how to tell Altair the truth.

Few people were on the street, but this conversation they needed to have was not likely to be fast or easy. Spotting a nearby bookstore that he knew also held a wine bar, Magnús made up his mind.

"Let's go in there. We need chairs and some kind of fortification." When Altair seemed about to protest, Magnús rested a hand on his shoulder. "Trust me just a little longer. Please."

Now Altair was the one to sigh, but he gave a sharp nod and followed.

Inside, the tables of blond wood, where customers sat with wine and perhaps a book, were mostly full. One empty table, though, stood well enough away from the shelves and the other patrons.

Leaning down, Magnús said in Altair's ear, "Will you grab that table, please? I'll get us something to drink."

Altair frowned at him. "If you disappear or walk out on me now, I'll, I'll...complain to your mother."

Magnús fought the urge to smile. "We can't have that, can we? I'll stay in plain sight the whole time."

Shortly, he joined Altair at the little table, a glass of red wine in each hand. Altair had taken a chair against the wall so he could keep an eye on Magnús, leaving a second chair with its back to the small crowd.

Unacceptable.

Magnús set down the glasses, then shifted his chair to sit looking out across the bar and bookstores. He darted a glance sideways at Altair, then mentally shrugged. He was about to let many, many cats out of the bag, so what was one more? He sketched two quick sigils in the air, one to turn away any human who would approach—the same he'd used on the children at Sundhöllin—and one to keep the sounds of their conversation from traveling. As he muttered the words to power his spells, he felt the young man tense beside him.

"What is that?" Altair demanded, both awe and curiosity shading his voice. He gestured at the runic symbols that Magnús could see glistening in thin air but that no human could detect.

That no human *should* be able to detect, he amended, since Altair was clearly staring right at them.

"You can see the sigils?"

"Of course, they're right there." Altair waved impatiently at them. "But what are they? How do they just stay there in the air without any surface?" He glanced around quickly. "And why is nobody else freaking out about them like I am?"

Magnús chose to tackle the last question first. "Because you are not like any of them. You're like me, but...not exactly."

"Is this more about elves?" Altair gave a roll of his eyes. "Because I'm too old for—"

"We call ourselves huldufólk," Magnús interrupted. "The hidden ones. Elf is what the Vikings called us when they first came from Norway."

Altair stared at him for a moment, clearly waiting to be told what the joke was. Instead, Magnús nudged a glass of wine toward him, then took a sip of his own.

"I'd like to tell you another story," he said when Altair had reluctantly sampled his own glass. "Long, long ago, Óðinn the Allfather fashioned the first man and woman from two trees. With his brothers Vili and Vé, Óðinn bestowed life on them, and named them Askur and Embla. Yes, I'm aware that sounds like Adam and Eve. Don't interrupt."

"I wasn't going to," Altair said sulkily but took a larger gulp of his wine.

Magnús continued his tale and concluded the same way his

tutor had. "From those children came my race, the huldufólk. From the other children, all humans are descended."

Altair pushed aside his glass. "So, can I say something now?"

"Not if it's to call my story kjaftæði. It's a myth we have in Iceland, not unlike origin stories of humans and nonhumans the world over. Is it fact? Probably not, but who can say? It is true in its most essential points."

Magnús leaned closer, holding Altair's gaze steadily. "My people can turn invisible at will. We can speak directly to each other's minds, and we have magic. Like that," he said, gesturing to the two sigils drifting in the air.

"Wait, you speak with your minds? Like, telepathy?" Altair was frowning now.

"That word works, I suppose."

"Is that what happened when we ran into your mother? You were, uh, telepathing or whatever? Because I thought I could hear words. Something about a spade-o-mur."

"Spádómur," Magnús said automatically, though he was shocked. "It means prophecy." He'd suspected Altair might be able to learn the mind-to-mind skill, but not that he already had a bit of it. Before he could comment further, Altair inhaled sharply and sat up straight. His eyes were glassy, face flushed, and his breathing was harsh.

"Is that what you've been doing all along? Reading my mind?" Altair pushed back from the table, rocking his wine glass. "It's been obvious you were keeping secrets, but this is too much. You aren't from the University at all, are you?"

Well damn, which question to answer first? He opted for one that he hoped would keep Altair from storming away.

"I came looking for you because you are in grave danger."

The protest in Altair's mouth died away when he snapped his jaw shut. He blinked. "Uh, what?"

"I don't have all the answers yet," Magnús said, leaning

forward. "There is a witch who foretold you are bringing something called the Bishop's Shackles to the Black Priest. You will die unless I am there, too."

He omitted the part about his own doom following if Altair lived. A human just learning about the hidden world did not need that additional burden. He waited for his words to sink in, for Altair's next question.

The last response he expected was for Altair to knock over the table, wine, and chairs as he fell to the ground in violent convulsions.

Magnús threw himself down, trying to cushion Altair's head as he thrashed. Patrons raised cries of alarm, and chairs scraped across the floor as people jumped to their feet.

"I'm calling One-One-Two," a woman nearby yelled in American-accented English, holding up her phone. Magnús barely heard her. Emergency Services wouldn't be able to help Altair.

«Bryndís!» he called out frantically, praying she was still nearby after her meeting with the queen. «It's Altair. I think he's being attacked by magic.»

The seizure had Altair kicking his feet on the ground. Magnús tugged at the collar of Altair's sweater to loosen it as much as possible and looked frantically for something to put in Altair's mouth to prevent him biting his tongue.

What to do next? His mind was blank with panic.

"Put him on his side," advised the woman who'd called Emergency Services. Magnús nodded gratefully and repositioned Altair as gently as he could. He held the small, lithe body in his arms, wracking his brain for a spell that could help. Nothing came to him, and he wanted to weep in frustration.

A moment later, a hand touched his shoulder, and he heard his mother's voice.

"Thank you so much. We have it from here," Bryndís said. He looked up gratefully, in time to see Bryndís gesture at the helpful woman with her fingers and whisper a spell. The woman and other gawking strangers turned away.

Bryndís crouched and laid a hand briefly on Altair's forehead, then grimaced and shook her head. "Powerful sorcery. My son, no human doctor will stop this. We must get him to Hamarinn."

"That's more than two hours on foot," he protested.

"Altair will be dead in that amount of time." Bryndís added firmly, "You must open the Hidden Ways."

Magnús darted his glance around the bookshop. "Here? Everyone will see!"

"I'll distract the humans." Bryndís sounded confident. "This is your gift, my son. Perhaps it's why the Nornir chose you."

She turned to face the crowd still milling uncertainly about the store. A distant siren reached Magnús's ears, probably the Emergency Services team. Bryndís spread her hands wide and wove her spell, some sort of illusion mixed with memory alteration, well beyond Magnús's capability.

Trusting to her wisdom, Magnús rose to his feet, with Altair grasped tightly in his arms. "Hold on, little bird," he whispered and *pulled* hard from his core.

The magic of Álfheimur rose within him, then surged through his body. The power was so intense it burned from within. Light flared from his very bones and through his skin, sparkling off the walls and the overturned table. It coruscated up and down his body. Wonderfully, Altair's thrashing eased. Perhaps the light was soothing the troubled human in his arms.

Filled with magic to the point of bursting, Magnús didn't even need to sketch a sigil. His mind formed the glyph, his lips released the spell, and reality parted before his eyes. The bookshop separated, as if painted on a curtain that was then drawn apart. Through the opening, he gazed upon the glory of Álfheimur and stepped through.

A vista of crystalline cliffs rose to either side of him, scintillating with captured light. The cavern ceiling of Hamarinn covered in sunstones, amazing though it was, seemed pale and colorless compared to the home of the ljósálfar, the light elves that his own people became when they left Miðgarður behind forever.

A path strewn with diamond dust led between cliff walls that shimmered so gloriously they almost sang. The melody of the light was welcoming and full of love that brought tears to Magnús's eyes. *Stay*, it crooned. *Your heart knows it is home.*

The distant sound of laughter told him where more of the light elves gathered. Part of his nature yearned to join them, as always. Even as it welcomed, though, the magic there threatened to consume him. To stay was to become fully ljósálfar, to have every trace of the mortal world burned away, leaving him unable to appear human on Miðgarður. The song of welcome, the laughter of his people... He had considered whether to stay, after Sigurjón's death.

The hypnotic song of magic made Magnús sway once more. Would it be so bad to remain? To leave Miðgarður to its fate? The Nornir had to be wrong about him; there were others who could take up the cause of saving humans.

Altair moaned softly in his arms. His body had stopped convulsing when they stepped into the Ways, but a fresh spasm made his closed eyes clench tightly, as if in pain. A human could not survive the light of Álfheimur for long. It burned away mortality, and a human was pure mortal. Even the magic thing that lived in Altair might not be enough to preserve him.

As Magnús looked down at the small, fragile burden in his arms, a wave of affection swelled in him. Altair was being used as a pawn by forces of darkness. He deserved so much better. He deserved a full life, free of sorcery and menace.

Tamping down the impulse to surrender to the light of his race's home, Magnús hurried along the diamond path. Without conscious thought for his steps or direction, he carried Altair to safety.

Álfheimur was smaller than Miðgarður, such that a step in the elf-realm could cover miles in the human's world. He had heard the fairy tale of the seven-league boots, which took the wearer twenty-one miles in a single stride; perhaps the original storyteller had experienced something similar to what Magnús did. Mountains could be crossed in Miðgarður with a simple jump in Álfheimur.

He hurried no more than fifty paces, Altair held tightly in his arms, when he wove his spell again. With the unerring accuracy that was part of his gift, the curtain spread open to reveal they'd reached Bryndís's meeting hall in Hamarinn.

He stepped through with a cry, both for the pain burning him from within and for the wrench of leaving Álfheimur behind. Magic drained out of him. He sagged to his knees, careful still of the small burden in his arms. Gently, he stretched Altair on the stone floor before dropping to lay prone himself.

"Well done, my son," Bryndís said. He hadn't even realized she'd followed him into the Hidden Ways. She carried their jackets and Altair's satchel and gift bag.

With tired, blurring eyes, he looked up at her. "Help Altair," he croaked out, weak as a kitten. And then he slept.

CHAPTER

TWENTY

When Magnús woke, he was lying on a thick mattress, in a chamber lined with wooden planks. White curtains hung at the window, a light blanket covered him, and his head rested on a soft pillow. It took a moment for him to recognize his old room in Bryndís's longhouse.

Ólafur sat next to the bed in a plain chair of natural wood. His long hair was still pulled back messily into a man-bun; he idly tugged on a loose strand as he read from a human magazine. The part of the cover Magnús could see said something about the "Reykjavik hipster metal scene."

Magnús's throat was dry, his lips parched like he'd been in the sun all day with no water. But he had a more burning need to address first.

"Altair?" he managed to say.

Ólafur looked up quickly and gave him a grin as he tossed his magazine aside. Magnús felt a weight lift from him right away.

"Your Falcon is doing well," Ólafur said. "That was a ballsy move, breaking the First Covenant. But you didn't handle the big reveal very well, Cousin. Surely you could have found an easier way to unload all our secrets."

Disgruntled, Magnús adjusted his pillows to prop himself up better. He was still weakened; opening the Hidden Ways took so much magic from him that he felt hollow. The weakness made him peevish, so he snapped, "I suppose you could have done better, with your keen insight into human minds."

"Well, I would have known not to tell him his life was in danger right off." Ólafur seemed unruffled, which made Magnús even more irritated. "How about just showing him a bit of magic first, to ease him into it?"

"He saw the sigils I was using. What more *should* I have shown?"

"Turn invisible for him? Whistle up a rain shower or cast a glamour?" Ólafur shrugged. "Lots of ways to get him curious and invested before dropping a truth bomb about the prophecy."

"He told you about that, huh?" Magnús hated to admit his cousin was right. He could have handled it all a lot better.

"Actually, no. I had to go into his memories to see what triggered the seizure."

Magnús bolted upright. "You went into Altair's mind?" Outrage and a surge of possessiveness made him forget his weakness. He trusted himself to go no deeper than necessary, but Ólafur might not share his scruples. "Of all the—"

"Chill, Magnús." Ólafur raised a hand to gesture for calm. "Bryndís needed me to read him so we could save his life. I went only to his surface memories."

The door opened just then. Bryndís herself walked in, nodded a greeting to Ólafur, and sat on the edge of the bed. "How are you feeling, my son? Are you recovered from opening the Ways?"

"Getting there, my mother. I don't think I'll be doing any big magics for a few days yet."

Bryndís laid her hand on top of his. "In all my years, I have never met one like you, who can enter and leave Álfheimur at will." She almost sounded proud of him, which made Magnús blink. "For most who choose to live on Miðgarður, the journey back to the world the Æsir created for us comes once. When the burden of long life grows heavy, or the allure of observing mortals fades, Freyja herself arrives to open the Ways and usher that álfur home. None ever returns. But you, my son...you are remarkable."

Magnús blushed. "I wouldn't say I can do it at will. The cost is high, and every time, I feel the temptation to remain."

"No gift from the gods comes without a price."

"How were you able to cure Altair?"

"Ah. We have not cured him." Bryndís withdrew her hand and rose from the bed's side.

Magnús stiffened in alarm and threw off the light covering over him. He swung his legs to the floor. "I thought he was all right. You said he was." This was hurled accusingly at Ólafur, who bristled.

"I said he was doing well for now. Simmer down, Cousin."

"If you are rested enough, come meet with us," Bryndís said. "Altair is in the library. I thought some light history of our race might answer the questions you did not have time to address."

"I was going to," Magnús muttered as he stood. "He seized first, remember?"

In the hall where they'd gathered to meet Diwata early that morning, a fire blazed in the hearth at one end of the chamber. A wooden chair, lined with a brightly colored cushion, sat near the fire. The witch sprawled sideways across it, a pile of books stacked next to the chair.

Without looking up from her book, Diwata gestured at a small basket on a sideboard. "I made kleinur for the shop today and brought the extra. Help yourself."

Magnús couldn't resist reaching into the basket to retrieve one of the sweet, fried dough treats and bite into it. "So good," he sighed. Diwata might be vaguely irritating, but she was a damn fine baker. He went for a second, but Ólafur knocked his hand away.

"That one's mine," Óli whispered fiercely.

Bryndís glided toward her large, carved chair but paused to look over Diwata's shoulder at whatever book she was reading. She nodded. "Ah yes, I remember that case. The poor man was no witch, just a natural wolf-dreamer. We tried to help him, but the witchfinders were too set on taking his property. They burned him at the stake."

"Barbarians," Ólafur murmured. "Dee, do your books mention that some of the huldufólk were captured and killed in those times as well? Magnús and I were too young then to be allowed near the areas where the fervor was strongest, but my brothers Lars and Vörður went when they could try to get some of the witches to safety. Lars's friend Jökull was one of those the hunters captured and then burned."

Magnús was troubled at the thought of a friend of Lars's being mistaken for a witch and murdered. He didn't want even a moment of sympathy for the murderer of Sigurjón. Ruthlessly, he squashed his own curiosity and instead asked Diwata, "What are you looking for in these books? Maybe I can help."

Diwata sighed. "The witches council is about as up to date as the last century. They let me access their records, but it turns out nothing is stored in a way that's, you know, actually useful. All they have are bound volumes of gossip and whining, with smatterings about useful events. I snagged a set, and Óli helped me transport them here." She gestured widely to the pile. "I started with the trials, but feel free to dive in wherever you want."

Before Magnús could reply, a gesture of Bryndís's hand drew everyone's attention to where she sat on her large chair. Diwata seated herself properly, and both Magnús and Ólafur took chairs at the central table. Silence fell except for the crackle of the fire, and Bryndís began.

"First, allow me to say I have met with Queen Hildur. She has heard of you, my child," Bryndís said to Diwata, "and honors the favor shown to you by the Nornir. She will meet with her captains promptly to marshal our forces."

Diwata looked down at her lap, but a pleased smile stretched her lips. "Thank you, Lady Bryndís," she murmured.

"Let us discuss Altair Fálkason next. Magnús, I agree with your choice to reveal our world. I will stand with you if the queen or any other questions your actions."

"Thank you, Mother," Magnús said, relieved and also surprised to find himself moved by her support.

"While you rested," she continued, "I have told these two what I know from when we met earlier in town. Altair's convulsions eased when you arrived here, but whatever sorcerous ailment he suffered still had control of him. It was I who asked Ólafur to enter Altair's mind for clues. Ólafur?" She nodded at him.

"Right." He sat up straight under Bryndís's gaze but faced Magnús, hands folded on the wooden table. "As I said, I went as gently as I could through his memories. I heard you tell him the myth of our creation and so forth. He was furious because he thought you were lying or tricking him, and he was determined to leave. In his memories, I could tell you said something else to him about prophecy and the threat to his life, but the words were lost. Instead, a, a *miasma* of some kind welled up and sucked Altair in."

Magnús raised a hand to his own head. "I think something similar happened earlier, but I'd almost forgotten." He tried to open himself to share his own memory, but he was too drained of magic. "Mother, if you would..."

Bryndís nodded, her eyes shone blue, and he felt the brush of her mind against his. Then she connected him to Ólafur and

Diwata as well. He revisited the conversation as he'd walked with Altair, when they'd been discussing Iceland, and it seemed as if Altair's own memory was altered in some fashion.

Diwata nodded speculatively. "That's in line with what I guessed. This spell Altair is under, the sorcery that the Nornir warned us about. I think it's a kind of, of *snare* that catches his mind when he gets too close to the truth. Well, close to whatever 'truth' it is that the sorcerer behind this wants to conceal. When you questioned him too intently, the spell took hold. Then when you told him about the prophecy, it triggered again."

"Why was it so much worse the second time? Did I do that, by telling him his life was in danger?"

"Yes," Ólafur said, at the same time Diwata said, "No."

They looked at each other in confusion for a moment, then Diwata shook her head emphatically. "It wasn't that, Óli. Well, not exactly. Magnús's ham-handedness triggered the spell, that's true. But the seizure. That was Altair's own magic fighting back."

Ham-handed and *Altair's own magic* warred in Magnús's brain. Concern for Altair won out. "So, he does have magic? Do you know what he is?"

Disappointingly, Diwata shook her head. "Not yet. As far as I can tell, he's human, not huldufólk or gnome or dwarf or any other supernatural being I've heard about. He's not a witch either. But somehow, he has a powerful magical core."

Bryndís steepled her fingers and leaned back in her massive chair. "Diwata and I agree, this sorcery that binds Altair most likely conceals his nature from himself and from others. But the magic is strong and is trying to free itself. If it *is* a power of this country, as seems logical, then we would guess setting foot in Iceland has awakened it."

Magnús frowned as he tried to process that. "So we're supposing a sorcerer put Altair under a spell and then, what, sent him here with this Bishop's Shackles thing?" Bryndís nodded once. "But if the sorcerer knows enough about Altair to control his magical nature, whatever it may be, wouldn't they know the magic might break free?"

Diwata sighed. "That's another thing I'm trying to research. What kind of spell could cage powerful magic but is subtle enough to rewrite Altair's memories to avoid him learning the truth. This is beyond anything I've ever heard of. It's the kind of magic reputed to be contained in the Rauðskinna."

"What is that?" Magnús asked.

"The Red Book is a notorious grimoire crafted hundreds of years ago," Diwata said. "Supposedly its spells were inscribed in golden letters on red parchment."

"This spell sounds evil, whatever it may be," Ólafur said, a look of distaste on his face. "Meddling with a human mind that way, not to mention distorting or enslaving a magical nature. That is black magic, to be sure."

"Black magic for the Black Priest?" Bryndís said thoughtfully.

"A Black Priest...from the Black School?" Diwata sat up straight and gave Bryndís a wide-eyed look.

The elf woman inhaled sharply. "Well-thought, child. Yes, the Black School. Now you say it aloud, that is indeed one of the whispers I heard in your prophecy."

"Is the Black School one of the human universities?" Ólafur asked.

Diwata turned to him eagerly. "No, silly. Do you know the legends of Sæmundur? When he was a young man, he left Iceland with two friends, looking for work. Was it Paris they went to? I don't remember it all, but somehow, he and his friends were lured into a school. The Black School, run by the Devil, to teach the dark arts."

"We seem to be onto something," Magnús said cautiously. "But what were you saying about Altair?"

Bryndís leaned forward and rested her palms on the table,

thumbs together. "Diwata and I have been unable to counter or remove his enchantment directly. With what Ólafur learned of Altair's trigger, though, we speculate that memory is the key to suppressing his seizure. We altered his recollection slightly so that your conversation with him ended right before you disclosed the prophecy."

"You did what?" Magnús blurted, angry now.

Diwata shot him a look. "Calm down. It was the least invasive way we could come up with to deal with your fuck-up."

Ólafur bit back a chuckle, and Bryndís looked disapproving. Still, Diwata's words got through to Magnús. He leaned back in his chair heavily with a huff.

"Fine. I messed up. But now what?"

"Now we must keep him from suffering another episode until we can discover how to lift his enchantment."

Magnus gaped. "Wait, you mean I have to keep him safe and alive for two more days, but I can't let him know why I'm hanging around him?"

"Exactly, Cousin." Ólafur sounded far too cheerful about the impossible challenge facing Magnús. "Which is why it's a lucky thing he has a crush on you. You should be able to keep him in your sights, day and night, no problem."

Magnús narrowed his eyes. The idea that he would play upon Altair's feelings, even for the man's own protection, nauseated him. Altair was kind, bright, and charming, but also unworldly and—through no fault of his own that Magnús could see— trapped in a sorcerous undertaking that could kill him.

He snarled at Ólafur. "Just seconds ago, you were bemoaning spells to manipulate minds. You know, Cousin, sometimes I am reminded that you are Lars's brother."

Diwata sucked in a shocked breath. "Savage," she muttered.

Ólafur turned beet-red. "Always Lars. If you weren't so in love with your own tragedy, maybe we could have all been a family again when he returned from exile."

"Enough," Bryndís commanded, her voice cracking like a whip. "My son, no one is suggesting you manipulate Altair. You simply must find a way to be at his side without telling him the complete truth. For his own protection."

She turned her gimlet stare upon Ólafur, who paled. "And you, my brother's son, will recall that your gift from the gods to see what humans are thinking is not a license to judge or to use them."

"Yes, Lady Bryndís," Ólafur said, chastened.

Taking a deep breath, Magnús bowed his head to his cousin. "Óli, I am sorry for what I said, and for what I implied. You sided with me during my investigation of Lars, you were a friend to Sigurjón, and I was wrong to speak to you like that."

Ólafur met his eyes, then solemnly returned the bow. "And I was wrong to speak frivolously of a matter I should know would pain you. I am sorry, Magnús."

"Child," Bryndís said to Diwata. "The other matter."

"Oh, right." Diwata rummaged among her books and pulled out a piece of paper. "Lady Bryndís and I aren't getting very far yet on understanding the spell on Altair. But we did find this, so we have a place to start."

She pushed the paper in front of Magnús. "There's a kind of tattoo on the hollow of Altair's neck. It was hidden by magic, which has to mean it's really important. So, we'll show this around to some other powerful witches and elves, to see if anyone has ideas on what it means."

On the paper was drawn a symbol, a rune of some kind apparently, though Magnús merely glanced at it.

Then he snatched the paper out of Diwata's hand.

"Rude," she muttered.

"This rune. I've seen it twice today!" Magnús blurted.

"Where?" Bryndís demanded.

"Early this morning, I found it written in elf-blood on the wall of a troll cave, though I didn't recognize it for a rune at the time. Then I saw it painted on the side of the hotel where Altair is staying. And now you tell me this same symbol is somehow engraved on Altair's skin."

He dropped his hands onto the table, the drawing still clutched in one fist. "The Black Priest, the Shackles, Altair...and the troll attacks on humans. I think it's all connected."

CHAPTER

TWENTY-ONE

ONE HUNDRED YEARS EARLIER

Magnús strode angrily across a stretch of land in the northeastern section of Iceland, steeling himself for the trial ahead. Along the main road of a small town, past human businesses connected with fishing and boat repair, he rehearsed his arguments, until Álfaborg came into sight.

All that humans could see was a mound of lichen-covered boulders in the middle of a green field, but—as with Bryndís's demesne—racial memory told the Icelanders who lived in the town that the area was special. Important. Few truly believed the queen of the huldufólk kept court in the center of their fishing village. Fewer still had knowingly met one of the huldufólk. But that hadn't stopped the town from capitalizing on their legends in a bid to attract some of the wealthy Europeans who boasted of touring the Nordic lands.

Magnús could feel the pulse of power from deep within Álfaborg as he climbed. Witches he knew averred that its boulders were at the convergence of several mystical ley lines. With his gift to open the Hidden Ways, he could sense that the barriers between Miðgarður, Álfheimur, and the rest of the Nine Realms were thin here.

He paused as he passed into Queen Hildur's vast underground realm. Unlike Hamarinn with its cavern roof covered in sunstones, Hildur had caused the ceiling of Álfaborg to resemble a star-filled sky. Midnight-blue stones, dotted with clusters of brilliant white diamonds, cast the hidden valley below into night that nonetheless showed the queen's palace in sharp relief.

Built of wood harvested before the humans and volcanic eruptions deforested Iceland, three round towers connected by thick walls sheltered a beautiful longhouse and the other structures of Hildur's court. Outbuildings, pens, and gardens teemed with activity as elves tended to their livestock and their crops. A waterfall at the far left of the cavern formed a pool and then a river that wended its way through the palace grounds and helped irrigate the bucolic setting. The scents of tilled earth and manure, rich with life and mixed with the smell of magic, filled the air.

It would all be lovely and moving, if Magnús were not here for justice and vengeance.

He hurried down to the valley floor and through the main gate of the protective wall. Surprisingly, Bryndís stood outside the queen's hall and held out a slender hand in invitation.

Magnús joined her, bowing his head as he took her hand. "I did not expect to see you here, my mother."

"I had other business with the queen and so I put off my return to Hamarinn until after this trial." Bryndís's fingers tightened on his. "My son, you know that I grieve for your loss. Yet I worry over the path you now tread."

"I don't know what you mean, Mother."

"My brother told me he offered manngjöld to the family of Sigurjón, and to you, in compensation for Lars's actions and in accordance with human law. But you rejected his gold and insist on Lars being tried as if he had killed one of our people."

Magnús growled. "This was no prank or mischief that Lars committed, Bryndís. He maliciously set out to lead Sigurjón to his death, then he tried to cover up his crimes. The bastard wanted to hurt me and in the process destroyed a pure and innocent life. That the life was human does not signify. Only the need to see Lars punished keeps me from seeking the relief of Álfheimur."

Uncharacteristically, Bryndís ran her hand over Magnús's hair and let it rest on his shoulder. "Ah, my son," she sighed. "This is the path I mean. The vengeance that burns in your heart will not be satisfied at any outcome today unless the queen orders Lars to be killed, which she will not do."

Magnús stiffened and stepped backward, away from Bryndís's touch. "Have you and the queen already discussed the matter in full, then? Are you like the rest of our people who chide me for pursuing this course, or who tell me Sigurjón would have died anyway? Has Hildur already decided what reprimand will be sufficient for the loss of a mere mortal?"

"*Queen* Hildur keeps her own council, my son, and follows the laws she herself set down." Bryndís's tone was quelling. "She has agreed to hear your case against Lars. I would do nothing to sway her or to interfere with your quest for justice."

"But you think she will not punish Lars as she should?" Magnús could feel his temper rising, even though he knew he was close to words that would truly offend.

Bryndís clasped her hands before her and held herself still, a sign she was hurt or angry. Yet her tone was even when she answered.

"Queen Hildur will be just, Magnús, but she will not tolerate disrespect. If you wish a fair hearing in Sigurjón's name, then you must control this anger you feel toward all huldufólk. That is the best advice I can give, as your gyðja and as your mother."

He knew he should listen to Bryndís's counsel. And he tried, with all his might. When he entered the audience chamber set aside for such purposes as this trial, he clenched his fists at the sight of Lars with a sneer on his lips, slouched indolently in a wooden chair. His clothing was finely made but loose and even a bit wrinkled, as if Lars had no troubles or care about the proceedings.

Queen Hildur was arrayed soberly on her throne of judgment. Her black hair—an unusual trait in their kind—was pulled back from her stern and ageless face. She listened without interruption as Magnús detailed his investigation into the uncanny nature of Sigurjón's fall to his death from a cliff he knew well, on a sunny afternoon. He relayed evidence from several huldufólk of Lars mocking humans. and working malicious magic on several people. Then, most damning of all, he presented a witness who heard Lars boasting of his trick, how he had drawn a mist over Sigurjón's eyes and called to him in a voice that sounded like Magnús until he led the young human right over the cliff's edge.

His case presented, Magnús began his summation. "Queen Hildur, the evidence that Lars, son of Berkir, committed these acts is irrefutable. His crimes must not go unpunished. By Your Grace's just laws, harm wrought by one elf upon another of our kind is punished most severely. An act of deliberate violence that leads to death is grounds for execution.

"But did not the Æsir create mankind as they created the huldufólk? Are mortals less beloved by Óðinn Allfather than our immortal race? I beg Your Grace to consider that the willful murder—yes, I say murder—of any human by one of us is an affront to the gods and should be punished no less severely.

"Though Lars be my kin, I ask the ultimate sanction be imposed. Not for my sake as one who loved a mortal but for the sake of the human Sigurjón, a child of the gods, whose life was stolen through cruelty and malice."

A hush fell through the audience chamber as Magnús concluded. The queen's deep sigh seemed loud in the silence, and her face was troubled.

"We hear your grief and your plea, Magnús, son of Bryndís." Hildur's sonorous voice effortlessly reached every ear. "How do you answer these charges, Lars, son of Berkir?"

Lars rose to his feet from the chair in which he had slouched. With a smirk aimed at Magnús, he said, "Truly, my cousin need not have bothered taking up Your Grace's time with that tedious recitation of evidence. I do not deny it. The human named Sigurjón annoyed me, so I repaid him in the manner our kind have always responded to an insult or wrong. I cursed him with blindness, I taunted him with his lover's voice, and I left it to the Nornir to guide his steps. That those steps led over the edge of a cliff is a sign that the gods do not care as much for mortals as my dear cousin would have Your Grace believe."

Magnús clenched the arm of his chair so fiercely it creaked. The awareness of a dagger in his belt burned in his mind.

"So you admit that your actions were deliberate and led directly to the death of the mortal," Queen Hildur said. It was not a question. "How do you respond to the call for punishment?"

Lars shrugged, his hands held wide as if in bewilderment. "Your Grace, if the huldufólk were to answer for the death of any mortal that crossed their path, this would be a land of corpses. With all appropriate deference, even Your Grace might be called to answer. We all recall the sad time in ages past when an evil spell took you from us and caused you to believe yourself mortal. Only on one night a year did the enchantment lift, and on that night, you were known to ride a mortal through the air like a steed to return to this place for a brief time. Many mortals died from the effort, before the enchantment was eventually undone and you were welcomed back by a grateful people."

Magnús leapt to his feet, teeth bared, one hand already on his hilt. "It is a false example you give, wretched Cousin. The Queen was under a spell, where you acted from malice. The mortals who died then owe their deaths to the witch who ensnared Her Grace."

"Enough." The voice of Hildur rang through the hall, silencing Magnús and Lars at once. "I have made my judgment."

Lars stiffened, while Magnús clenched his jaw. Silently, he offered a prayer to Týr, in His aspect as the god of justice rather than war. *May my words have reached the queen's heart to bring justice for Sigurjón, murdered so cruelly for spite.*

Hildur stared intently at Magnús, her eyes bright and penetrating. Her power to see into the hearts and minds of her people was the stuff of legend, so he had no doubt the queen had heard his prayer to Týr. Yet when she spoke, her first words dashed his hope.

"By the grace of the Æsir, I am called to serve as mouthpiece to wise Forseti, he who brings reconciliation with justice." The queen's voice resonated through her hall. "The god tells me that a burden of blood and honor lies between two of my people. Yet the burden will be increased, not diminished, if further blood be spilled.

"Magnús, your loss is great, but think on this. Had Sigurjón lived, his mortal span would have run out in seven or eight decades at most.

"Lars, I see your heart. It was spite and malice toward your kin that led you to this act. Magnús has no need of manngjöld, and I will not grant him payment in blood. The only coin you can spend, Lars, is Time.

"As you robbed Magnús of a mortal span with the human he loved, you are banished from our world for a like span of time. For a period of seventy-five years, the doors of every elf-home are closed to you. The light of Álfheimur itself, I cloud from your eyes. Walk the mortal world, share their lives, and learn the nobility that the knowledge of limited years brings to humans."

Bryndís emerged from behind a tapestry. Magnús had not even realized she'd be present. "As Your Grace decrees, so shall it be done," his mother said.

Beside him, Lars trembled in fury but dared not argue with his queen and with his gyðja. Still, the look he hurled at Magnús was full of promised violence.

Lars bowed stiffly with jaw locked and then strode to meet Bryndís where she gestured. She led him behind the tapestry, which, Magnús now realized, concealed a door.

Queen Hildur still had her eyes fixed on him, and he realized he was quivering with as much fury as Lars had shown. Fury and abject sorrow. He had failed Sigurjón twice: first when he didn't prevent Lars's cruelty, and again when he could not earn justice.

"Peace, Magnús," Hildur said, in a tone that was as much warning as advice. "You are not alone in loving the mortals of Miðgarður, and you are not the first elf to have lost one dear to your heart. While I was under the curse and forced to live as a mortal woman, I too loved a human man and bore him many children. The spell was lifted, and I regained my true nature, yet the love I found while enchanted did not fade. I visited my mortal family as often as duty allowed. I watched my husband age and die. I saw my children, and their children, pass away through accident, misfortune, or time."

Hildur rose from her throne and came down the few steps to stand before Magnús. At her small gesture, Magnús sank to his knees and bowed his head. The queen rested her hand lightly on his hair, then said, "I cannot—I *will* not—give you the vengeance you crave. Yet I will grant you a boon. What would you have from me, Magnús Bryndísarson?"

"Your Grace, I ask for your blessing to act on behalf of the mortals. In the name of Sigurjón and of Queen Hildur"—her fingers twitched at the order of those invoked—"I ask freedom to pursue justice and to protect the humans of Miðgarður from unnatural threats."

Hildur sighed. "Very well, with this limitation. You may act as your conscience directs in immediate peril of your own life or that of one you guard. Otherwise, you will bring matters involving the huldufólk to your gyðja or to me for adjudication."

She tightened her hand until she was almost pulling his hair. "Do you understand me, Magnús? You are a hand of protection, not of vengeance."

"Yes, Your Grace. I hear and I will obey."

CHAPTER

TWENTY-TWO

Altair nibbled at his thumbnail. He sat by a warm fire in a wood-lined room, but the room might have been anywhere. Was he even still in Reykjavik? No clue.

It was a large space, filled with books, scrolls, and other odd things Altair couldn't identify. He'd looked all over but could find no window or clock.

The woman who'd brought him from the bedroom in which he'd awoken called it the library, which made sense, but it wasn't like any library he'd been in before. The book she handed him was in English and seemed to be full of fairy tales. More of the bullshit Magnús had tried to feed him.

That thought sent him down a different track, one that made his heart pound in rising panic. Where *was* Magnús? Somewhere in this weird place, he supposed, but where were they? If they weren't in Reykjavik, how would Altair get to his meeting with the professor at the University of Iceland? What would happen if he were late? He needed Professor Sigmundsdóttir to like him; he couldn't afford to piss her off.

He'd probably been stewing for an hour before the door

opened and Magnús entered the library. Altair jumped up from his cushioned chair. He rushed over and impulsively threw his arms around Magnús.

"Oh, thank god. What the hell is going on? Where are we? What time is it?"

Magnús hugged him back for a moment but then stiffened. Altair realized what he'd done, invading the guy's personal space. He immediately dropped the hug and stepped back, his cheeks warming.

"Sorry about that. I'm just a little freaked out."

"Completely understandable," Magnús said. He rested a hand on Altair's shoulder. "I owe you an apology for not handling this all better. May I try again?"

When Altair hesitated, Magnús gestured at two people who had come into the library after him. "Altair Fálkason, may I present my cousin Ólafur and my...friend Diwata."

The man had reddish hair, shaved at the sides, with the rest pulled back into a man bun. He was dressed in a loose-fitting white shirt, with trousers tucked into boots. Unfairly, he was as tall, handsome, and runway-ready as Magnús.

The woman was shorter, about Altair's height, with black hair. Her skin was slightly darker than the porcelain-white of the two cousins. She wore jeans and a tee-shirt with an image and name of a band he didn't recognize. Her dark, almond-shaped eyes regarded Altair shrewdly.

The woman—did Magnús call her Diwata?—tossed a scornful look at Magnús as she stuck out her hand to Altair. "Yeah, I wouldn't say friends either. Hello, Altair. Welcome to Rivendell."

"Um, what?" A *Lord of the Rings* reference? Did this woman also believe in elves?

The other man—Ólafur?—smiled. "Yes, she believes in elves. But she's a smart-ass, too."

"Hey," Diwata protested, elbowing Ólafur in the gut.

Magnús frowned at his cousin. "Óli, please. Don't read Altair's thoughts without permission."

Ólafur blushed. "I beg your pardon, Altair. Strong thoughts on the surface of a mind are always clear to me, and sometimes I can't tell if they've been said aloud. Yours are particularly clear, for some reason."

Altair's head swam and his knees trembled. All of these people kept insisting elves were real and could read minds. Could they actually be telling the truth?

"Steady there, tourist," Diwata said, grabbing Altair's arm before he could fall over. "It's a lot to take in. I get it." She pulled him closer, the smell of yeast and sugar and spices enveloping Altair. The hug she gave him was comforting, and suddenly he missed his mom terribly. He hugged back, already feeling more calm.

"I didn't lie to you," Magnús said gently. "Well, not about this. Iceland is shared by many races other than human."

"Y-you mean, there's more than just elves?"

"Oh yes. Óli and me, we're related to the light elves. There are also dark elves, dwarves, gnomes, trolls, mermen, nyk—"

"And witches," Diwata interrupted.

Altair leaned his head back to look at her but didn't break away from the hug and home-like smells. "Witches?"

"'Fraid so. I'm human, but I have a, um, facility to use some of the power in Iceland. These dudes mainly have racial magic, meaning the huldufólk are able to do their parlor tricks with turning invisible and reading minds and shit like that just by being alive. Witches have to work at it."

"Don't sound so bitter, Dee." Ólafur laughed, in a way that sounded fond. "We know you work hard to master your craft, but you have to have some innate ability to even be trained. Isn't that right?"

"Point."

"And why are you all telling me this?" Altair asked. "I mean, assuming I believe you."

Magnús shook his head. "I'm sorry, but I can't explain to you yet."

Altair was confused, had no idea where he was, hadn't eaten in hours, and now this *elf* was throwing ridiculous stories at him but wouldn't tell him why.

"Can't, or won't?" He released Diwata and turned to face Magnús. "This is bullshit. I want to go back to my hotel, go to my meetings, and get out of this place."

"We'll let you two sort this out." Ólafur drew Diwata by her hand to the other side of the library.

"Will you let me explain, at least as far as I can?" Magnús asked.

With a huffy near-growl, Altair sat heavily in the chair he'd vacated by the fire. "This had better be good."

Magnús knelt on the floor and put a hand on the arm of Altair's chair. "First, do you believe me, that I'm one of the huldufólk?"

"Fine. You're an elf, you can turn invisible, and you read my mind in order to lie to me."

That made Magnús wince. *No, I will not feel bad. I'm not the one being jerked around here.*

"There is danger to Iceland," Magnús said slowly, sounding cautious. "It involves you, but we don't know how exactly. And there is a very good reason we can't explain more, but I need your trust for now. When the reason goes away, I will explain everything. Can you trust me that far?"

Altair crossed his arms again and stared at the elf. He wanted to say no. He wanted to stamp his foot and bitch until they took him to his hotel.

Oh, who was he kidding? He'd trusted Magnús instinctively from their first drive together. It made no sense, but neither did whirlpools forming in a public swimming pool, or air-writing Altair could see when no one else could, or people who claimed they were a witch.

"Fine," he said reluctantly. "I trust you. I don't like this, I don't know what you want from me, but I'll play along. *If* it doesn't interfere with my grant work."

"Thank you," Magnús said, bowing his head. "We're about an hour from your hotel. I propose we spend the night here in Hamarinn, and I'll take you back in the morning in enough time to get ready for your meetings."

"You promise I'll get to the University of Iceland by ten a.m.?" Altair demanded. "All right. So...do we spend the evening playing Twenty Questions while I try to figure out what's going on?"

Diwata laughed from the other side of the room. "The sass is strong with this one. We're going to get along just fine."

At that moment, the door opened again. Magnús's mother entered, bringing with her a scent of pine and morning mist hanging in a forest—

Stop this. I am not from here, I don't know these things.

Her hair was in a braid that hung forward over the shoulder of a long, green robe, embroidered in silver. Altair frantically tried to recall her name. It was lovely but really unusual...

"I am Bryndís, and you are welcome in my hall."

He rose from his chair and took the hands she extended, feeling their strength. "Th-thank you for your hospitality, uh, ma'am?"

Bryndís smiled kindly. "You might be hungry, after your ordeal. I've arranged supper for all of you."

She gestured to a side of the room. As Altair turned that way, the room seemed to ripple. A table stood where she indicated, loaded with plates, cups, and covered dishes.

Altair gaped. "Where did that table come from? I mean, thank you. But did it slide out of the wall? How does it work?"

Bryndís laughed lightly. "Perhaps I'll have time to explain one day. But for now"—she turned to Magnús—"I must meet with Queen Hildur and her captains. Please, enjoy your meal." With that, she swept out of the room.

Ólafur went to the table and began lifting covers. "Oh nice. Smoked lamb, plokkfiskur, skyr with lingonberries, horse loin—"

"Horse?"

Ólafur looked puzzled at Altair's shocked tone. "Well, yes. It's quite good. Do you not eat horse in America?"

"No," Altair said firmly.

"Well, how about fermented shark?"

"That stuff is gross," Diwata said, wrinkling her nose. "I don't know how anyone can eat hákarl."

"I don't care for it either." Magnús gestured for Altair to join them at the table. "Don't feel obligated to try anything that makes you uncomfortable. Plokkfiskur is basically cod fish with onions and mashed potatoes."

"I'll give it a try. But probably not horse."

The food was tasty and comforting despite its unusual textures and tastes. Altair even tried a sliver of hákarl but nearly spat it out at the strong taste like rotted cheese and... Was that urine?

"Oh my god," he said, revolted. Ólafur passed him a small glass with a clear liquid. Altair tossed it back, then nearly spat that out as well. He gasped at the burn in his throat.

"Brennivín," Ólafur told him with a grin. "The humans call it 'black death.'"

"What is that flavor?" Altair asked, mopping his mouth and the plate in front of him.

"Caraway," Magnús said, then emptied his own glass. "Sometimes they use dill, but I prefer this version."

When they'd finished dinner, two young-looking men—elves? —came in to deposit some books and also to clear the dishes away.

Altair followed the others as they found seats near the fireplace. Diwata sighed at the pile of books. "I need to keep going through these."

"What are you looking for?" Altair asked, the academic in him interested in spite of his confusion. "Can I help?"

"No!" the others all responded in unison, then looked at each other wryly.

"More of what I can't know about, huh? This is getting old."

"Just trust us a little longer," Magnús begged. He retrieved the book of stories Altair had been leafing through earlier. "These are legends about encounters between humans and our kind. Perhaps you'll enjoy these, now that you believe."

Altair tried to read while the others each took a book from Diwata's pile. They seemed to know what they were looking for and acted comfortable with each other. Altair fought back a bit of jealousy at the closeness, at the feeling of family. Even though Magnús and Ólafur sniped at each other a little, it was harmless, reminding him of time spent with some of his favorite foster brothers and sisters over the years.

Suddenly he missed Willa and Jason. Something inside him, though, warned that he wouldn't be able to tell them about the huldufólk and Diwata.

The crackle of the fire, the comfortable cushions under him, and the meal made him sleepy. His body clock was still pretty confused about the time change from Boston.

To stay awake, Altair got up and moved around the room. Diwata had a green-bound book open on the arm of her chair, and she compared something in it to the book she was reading. Curious, he edged closer to take a look.

He'd only caught a peek of thick lines of ink creating intricate patterns on each margin of the pages, when Diwata turned on him with a fierce scowl.

"Sorry, sorry!" he said, backing away.

Diwata grimaced. "No, I'm sorry. Witches are very possessive of their grimoires. I can't help being jumpy when it's exposed like this."

Ólafur glanced at her from where he tended the fire. "Be at ease. No one here wants to take your galdrabók. I promise."

"I know," Diwata muttered, cheeks red now. She crooked a finger at Altair. "Come on. You might as well take a look."

Crouching next to her chair, he looked at the green-bound book, open to a page with runic notations. From somewhere, he'd picked up the idea that "galdra" meant a magic spell. "Bók" likely meant book. So...

"Galdrabók. That means, uh, spell-book in English, right?"

"Exactly," Diwata said. "Or grimoire. I inherited this from my great-grandfather, who had it from his father. In the Philippines where my mother was from, magic is for women and men. But here, it's male-dominated."

She turned a few pages, murmuring as she pointed to various images. "This is to find treasure. This one is to protect a house from storms. This is for birthing lambs."

She stopped at a design that looked, to Altair, like a snowflake. With a mischievous gleam in her dark eyes, she said, "This one is an old spell to increase luck at fishing. What you do is write this design onto the skin of a black cat, with menstrual blood. Then—"

"Stop torturing Altair," Magnús chided. "He already apologized."

Altair grinned at Diwata. "Don't listen to him, it's really fascinating. Does it have to be the witch's blood? You said most witches in Iceland are men."

"Good point," Diwata said. "In the early years of Iceland, the settlement era, women practiced seiður. That is, ritual magic. Men who used it were treated like sissies generally."

"The Vikings kicked sand in their faces?"

"You got it. The manly men preferred galdur, kind of like incantations. They both used runes, though."

Altair leaned in again for another look at the book, his mind already trying to define magic as if it were a science.

"You said a cat's skin. Why not paper, or maybe parchment? Wait, don't answer if I'm getting too much up in your trade secrets."

"It's fun to talk about," Diwata said. "What I write my spells on can be just as important as the runes. Like, if I want to protect a person, I write on their own skin. If I want to give someone luck for fishing, a piece of driftwood helps the magic."

"You said your magic is different from Magnús's and Ólafur's?"

"Witches don't have innate magic, like these guys have invisibility," Diwata said. "Do you know about the Nine Realms?"

"Magnús explained a little about it. And I played *God of War*, saw the Marvel movies, that kind of thing," Altair admitted sheepishly.

"*God of War* was awesome, wasn't it?" Ólafur said. "Of course parts of it were way wrong, but we spent hours on it. Right, Dee?" He grinned at Diwata, and they bumped their fists together.

Magnús rolled his eyes. "While the children play, I'll explain. Each of the other Nine Realms touches Iceland in some way, and beings of that race can draw from their home world's magic. We huldufólk draw our power from Álfheimur, the world of the light elves. Our close kin are the dökkálfar, the dark elves. Their magic comes from Svartálfaheimur, and they have power over shadows. The dvergar, or dwarves, who live here draw magic from Niðavellir. They can move through solid stone and have astonishing abilities with metal and rock. And so on."

Diwata nodded. "Witches, though, are from here on Miðgarður. We learn to use some of the magic from each of the

Realms that leaks through. But we need galdur and seiður, runes and incantations, to do that. Get it?"

"I think so." Altair tapped a finger against his lips. "Actually, it sounds like one of the geothermal power plants. Natural heat and groundwater are used to produce steam that a turbine then turns into electricity. If I understand, the huldufólk can use the natural heat directly for various effects, but a witch needs a turbine, in this case, a spell."

"That is...surprisingly apt," Magnús said.

"But I wouldn't say that in front of the witches council," Diwata added with a grin. "They take themselves way too seriously."

"Can anyone, I mean, any human, learn to do your kind of magic?" Altair asked.

Ólafur shifted so his back was leaning against Diwata's chair. "No. We aren't exactly sure why, but most humans lack any ability to sense the magic and draw on it. The best theory is it has to do with blood lines. At some point in a witch's lineage, you could probably find someone got busy with one of the huldufólk or dökkálfar, and that intermingling introduced a recessive gene to use magic." Altair's surprise must have shown in his face, because Ólafur shrugged at him. "What? I sat in on some genetics courses at the University. It interests me because of my livestock breeding programs."

"Óli, enough," Magnús said sharply. "I think we're getting too close to...one of the problematic topics."

Altair huffed noisily. "Fine. So, magic from the Philippines. Is it the same as here in Iceland? Are there all the different Realms and races?"

Diwata shook her head. "The only Realm that touches the Philippines is Niflheimur, where the dead reside. Same for any country that practices what you'd probably call voodoo. In North America, you used to have giants and dwarves, because Jötunheimar and Niðavellir have gateways there. As far as the witches have been able to determine, though, Iceland is the only country that has connections to all of the other Realms and races."

Altair looked at Magnús. "That's what you and Bryndís meant this afternoon, when you said there are so many sources of power in Iceland."

"Yes, but I really think we're getting into dangerous territory. I know you don't like that—"

"It's for my own good." Altair sighed. "Fine. I need to sleep anyway. But you!" He pointed at Magnús. "You'd better keep your promise and explain everything before I leave Iceland in two weeks."

Magnús exchanged shifty looks with the other two, then said, "I promise you will know everything no more than three days from now."

CHAPTER

TWENTY-THREE

Early the next morning, Altair blushed furiously as he led Magnús through the door of his hotel. They'd stayed the night in—what did they call the place? Hammering or something like that—and he'd woken up in an oddly designed but deeply comfortable bed.

Now, in the morning, he couldn't help feeling that he was doing a walk of shame, though he had, sadly, nothing to regret. Back in the real world of Reykjavik, surrounded by people who were starting their day, the night at, at—oh, at *Hamarinn*—seemed unreal.

As he walked across the lobby with the tall, blond zaddy at his side, Altair's thoughts of *What if they think I picked Magnús up at a bar?* warred with a prideful *That's right, look at the amazing man I'm bringing to my room.* Then he laughed at himself: *Talk about a delusion.*

Magnús remained silent as Altair guided him to the elevator. They entered the car with a youngish couple, their suitcases and weary expressions suggesting they had just arrived in Iceland.

Magnús and Altair rode to the fourth floor with no conversation between them. Altair's mind was seething with questions, but he understood they were not the kind to blurt out in public.

As they walked down the hall, though, he murmured, "I'll really be fine. There's no need to see me to my room."

Magnús leaned close enough to say softly in his ear, "You've been attacked twice that I know of. I'd rather not take any chances."

The elf held up a hand before Altair could insert his key into the door lock. After a quick glance up and down the hallway, Magnús sketched a symbol on the door with his finger and muttered words in a melodic tone. Altair was starting to recognize more phrases, because he picked up words he thought meant "shelter" and "protection."

Magnús placed his palm flat against the door and waited a moment before giving Altair a sharp nod. He stepped out of the way, Altair inserted his card key and then let Magnús into his room.

He hadn't unpacked, since he was only going to be in Reykjavik for a few days. The duvet on the bed was wrinkled from his nap the day before, clothes were strewn haphazardly, and his towel had fallen to the floor after his hasty shower.

"Um, let me just straighten up..." Altair muttered, grabbing his towel to drape it on a hook.

Magnús shook his head, the stern look Altair was so familiar with back in place. "No need. You said you want to get to the University soon, I believe."

Altair sighed. "I do, meeting is at ten. Do you really need to go there with me?"

Magnús moved some clothes out of the way to sit on the edge of the rumpled bed. "Yes. We talked about this already."

"We talked about a lot of things, but so much of it still makes no sense."

He stepped into the bathroom, leaving the door partially open when he removed his clothes and got the shower started. He could only hope that Magnús's presence wouldn't interfere with the tours he was scheduled to take. The magical metaphor was interesting, but it was the science behind the geothermal technology Iceland employed he had to understand. Magic wouldn't get him his doctorate, or keep him living in Willa's apartment, or make his family proud of him.

From the bedroom, he heard Magnús moving around as he called out, "The huldufólk are real. You are not fully human. Something sorcerous is happening around you, and we need to know what. Is that so complicated?"

Altair snorted as he finished stripping and climbed into the shower. "You and your mother and cousin are elves. Ancient elves. You live in a fairy town that's lit up by magic. A witch bakes you bread. Yes, that's complicated."

Magnús pushed open the bathroom door and leaned against the jamb, ignoring Altair's squeak and frantic turn to hide his junk from view. "But you said last night you believe me, even though we can't safely explain more right now. Yes?"

"Could we talk about this when I'm done with my shower?"

"So prudish." Altair could hear the eye-roll in Magnús's voice, but he turned his back. Softly, he muttered, "I'm not ancient, though."

"Fine, just four hundred. That's not ancient, just...antique."

"Have it your way. But we still need to understand what you are."

"I'm just *me*." Altair scrubbed shampoo into his scalp with more force than necessary. This was all mysterious, unwelcome, and so, so frustrating. "Ordinary student. Nothing special at all."

"Apply your education, then," Magnús said. "You've seen us turn invisible and work magic. You can tell when I'm in your head—"

"So uncool. I'm still mad about that." Altair ducked his head to rinse.

"Noted. I'd point out, however, that you know now what that sensation in your head means. No one will be able to read your thoughts without you being aware of it."

"That's supposed to make me feel better?" Altair demanded as he finished his shower and turned off the water. "You told me a whole load of kjaftæði when you met me at the airport and while we were spending time together. All the while you were picking details from my head. How am I supposed to know what to believe?"

"I acknowledge your anger," Magnús said placidly, which infuriated Altair. "You have to understand that reading a human's mind isn't something I do lightly, or well."

"And you won't even tell me why I deserved the honor." He toweled himself dry roughly, getting more irritated as he thought about how many times he'd felt that tickle. God, had Magnús heard the inappropriate things Altair had thought about the elf?

"I can't tell you. There's a very good reason, and I've promised that when that reason no longer exists, I will explain."

"Dammit! You keep saying that," Altair exclaimed, throwing his wet towel around his waist. He stalked into the bedroom for the clothes he'd forgotten to bring into the bathroom with him. "This is infuriating. Look. I've got to get going to meet my advisor. If you want to come along invisibly, fine. Just..."

Magnús didn't seem to understand how important this grant was to Altair. People were waiting back in Boston, people with their expectations and their certainty they knew what was best for Altair. He *needed* them, in a way Magnús could never understand. Magnús's mother was some kind of royalty. He had friends, family, a home...*everything* that Altair wanted.

Altair closed his eyes and breathed deeply as he tugged on his clothes. Whatever was going on, it wasn't Magnús's fault.

He pulled his sweater on, turning as his head emerged from the neck hole to see Magnús watching him warily. "Please," Altair begged. "If you come to the university, remember how important this is to me."

Magnús said, "I understand. I hope you understand me, too. I want to keep you safe from whatever is happening to you."

Altair zipped his pants, then sat on the edge of the bed. One shoe dangled loosely from his hand as he stared at the floor, unwilling to meet Magnús's eyes.

He had wondered, as soon as he learned about Magnús reading his thoughts, whether the elf had been manipulating him. Perhaps the sense of safety he felt around Magnús wasn't genuine? But every fiber of his being resisted that interpretation. Whatever the hell was going on, he still knew in his very soul that Magnús would keep him safe.

"I believe you," Altair whispered.

He looked up at Magnús, their eyes locking. Something wordless built between them, something that drew him to this man— *well, this elf*—and through him, to this country.

Magnús dropped to a crouch, resting on his heels before Altair. He extended a hand carefully until it landed on Altair's knee. "Whatever your heritage turns out to be, you are a part of the land. Someone in your past came from Iceland, and that means at least a part of you belongs here as well."

Altair shook his head. "I don't think so. Iceland is beautiful, but I'm terrified. Voices in my head, whirlpools, hidden valleys, elves... This isn't my life. I'm an engineering student. I'm going to build power plants back in the States someday."

He *wanted* to say that meeting Magnús was also the most wondrous thing that had ever happened to him, but that was ridiculous. What could someone who looked like Magnús, who was four hundred frickin' years old, ever see in Altair?

"Maybe"—Altair swallowed hard—"maybe I should just go home. Now. Today."

But he couldn't, could he? Walking away from the grant meant walking away from his Boston life. Walking away meant leaving Magnús behind, too...

Ice-blue eyes stared into his, and Altair waited for the tickle that he now knew signified his mind was being read. Some small part of him even wanted that, to have Magnús know the crazy things Altair thought and felt but could never say.

No tickle came, and he accepted, with mixed feelings, that Magnús was keeping his promise to stay out of Altair's thoughts.

After long moments, Magnús rose to his feet and looked around the hotel room. His voice seemed slightly hoarse as he said, "If you aren't going to leave Iceland, we'd better get you to the University."

"Right." Altair finished tying his shoes, then stood to gather things he needed for the meeting with Professor Sigmundsdóttir. He emptied his satchel to repack it more neatly. Some maps from his suitcase joined his laptop, his binder of materials on geothermal plants, and *the thing*, all placed back into his satchel, along with his notebook.

"I'm ready," Altair said, turning around.

"What did you just put into your bag?" Magnús asked, frowning.

"Just maps, my binder, laptop, and notebook. Why?"

"I think—"

At that moment, Altair's phone started ringing. It was the tone he'd set for Willa, so he quickly accepted the call.

"Hi, you're up so early! What is it, about three thirty there?"

"I just want to make sure you're ready for your meeting at the University," Willa said in his ear. "This is so important for you."

Altair chuckled. "I know. You've been drumming it into my

head for weeks. But yes, I'm all set." His eyes flicked to Magnús, who was trying and failing to look as if he wasn't listening avidly to the conversation. "The, uh, driver the University sent for me is here, so there's no way I'll be late."

"You should be sure to mention the driver to Professor Sigmundsdóttir when you meet her," Willa said, her tone sounding suspicious. "I'm surprised they went to the trouble."

"I'll say thank you, of course." Altair rolled his eyes and gave a goofy grin to Magnús. Willa was such a big sister, always checking up on him, making sure he presented himself at his best.

After a few more minutes of chatting, he let Willa hang up. He pulled on his heavy jacket and the mittens Magnús had lent him, swung his satchel over his shoulder, and made sure he had his room key. Magnús still watched him intently, puzzlement on his face.

Altair crooked his head. "What? Is my hair messed up or something?"

"Indulge me, please. Tell me again what you have in your satchel."

"I told you, just a binder of power plant specs, my computer, and a notebook."

Magnús narrowed his eyes slightly. "I saw you put something else in there, something that...*felt* wrong to me."

Altair snorted. "That's crazy. C'mon, I need to get going or I'll be late. Please, Magnús. I know you're trying to help me, but I can't miss this appointment." In fact, he felt his heartbeat ratchet up at the thought. His voice sounded strange to himself: tight, and even breathless. He realized he'd shoved his satchel farther behind him, blocking the view with his body.

Magnús held out a hand, palm up, in a placating gesture. "I understand. We'll leave right now."

Altair noticed when Magnús darted another look at the

satchel. Why was he obsessed with that? It contained *nothing* important. Altair was quite sure of that, and they had no time to look in it together anyway.

Before his palpitations could turn into a full-blown panic attack, he pulled open the hotel room door and all but rushed to the elevator.

TWENTY-FOUR

Magnús opened the passenger door to the Renault he'd borrowed to drive Altair back to his hotel and then take him to his appointment.

The car's owner was a human woman, Ingrid something-or-other, who lived in Hafnarfjörður and conducted "elf walks" for tourists. The last time he'd encountered one of her tours, he'd been amused enough to follow along invisibly for a few blocks. Ingrid had told stories about elf churches, elf celebrations, and a ghost story or two. None were true, but the tourists were fascinated. Magnús had made himself visible and walked past her; she'd caught his eye, done a double take, and then bowed her head respectfully. But she didn't say a word to her customers about the fact they'd just encountered one of the huldufólk.

Ingrid wouldn't mind the loan of her car, Magnús was certain. His concern was for the human seated next to him. He could see no way to persuade Altair to leave Iceland, so Magnús would continue to shadow him night and day until the new moon.

When he got behind the steering wheel, he noticed Altair shift his satchel farther away from Magnús, between himself and the car door. He didn't even seem to be aware of the motion.

Every instinct in Magnús cried out to look in the satchel, but he'd recognized the danger signs in Altair. The elevated heart rate, near-panicked breathing, flushed face...

He considered probing Altair's memories, to see how he recalled loading his satchel, but he'd promised not to do so without Altair's consent. Besides, Magnús's last encounter with the dark, sinister presence watching the human made that a very bad idea.

Magnús would have to watch for an opportunity to look in the satchel.

They drove through the morning traffic in silence for a few miles. Magnús had a bet with himself about how long Altair could keep that silence up.

"Have you been to the energy school at the University before?" Altair asked about three minutes in. When Magnús shook his head, he added, "How do you know where you're going then?"

"It's part of my gift. I just have to name or even think of a place, and I know exactly how to get there."

"Like, any place?"

"Yes."

"Does it have to be real? I mean, does it have to be a spot with geographic coordinates? Or could you say, 'Take me to the best restaurant near here,' or 'I want to know where Altair is'?"

"This is magic, not Google," Magnús said. "My talent works with specific points. Mappable, I suppose you could say. I don't have to have been to the spot."

"I'd like that talent. I get lost in Boston all the time."

They pulled into the University of Iceland parking lot. "Do you know the person you're meeting today, or what you'll be doing?"

"Just her name and reputation. Professor Milton arranged the introduction. Ellen Sigmundsdóttir is world-renowned for her geothermal studies and for the impact of projects on plant life." Altair consulted some papers from his satchel. "We're looking for... uh, yes, that's it, over there." He pointed at a building.

Magnús parked in a convenient spot close to the building indicated. With the satchel opened, he leaned over quickly for a look. Altair's laptop, some file folders, a small book with a pink, floral cover—

The book! That was the source of the feeling of wrongness he detected when he touched the satchel. What in all the Realms...?

A noise grew quickly in Magnús's ears then, rising from a hum to a sound like an enormous hive full of angry bees. Darkness closed in from the corners of his eyes. *Is this what fainting is like...?*

Everything was quiet, calm. Normal. Magnús blinked blearily at Altair. What had they been talking about? He had the sense of missing something important, but he couldn't imagine what it was. After all, he and Altair were just sitting in the car, waiting for Altair's appointment. The black satchel was closed and clutched in Altair's hands; nothing unusual there, since Altair tended to hold the bag as if it contained gold instead of just his laptop. That was probably related to Altair's anxiety over his dissertation studies.

"I said, that's the building over there." Altair indicated a nearby building, and Magnús nodded dazedly.

He shook off the momentary confusion, then turned to face Altair before the human could unlatch his seat belt. "I want to come in with you."

"But why? What's going to happen on a college campus? And you admitted you weren't really hired by the University, so I don't know what I'd say to Professor Sigmundsdóttir."

"I'll go in unseen, don't worry about that. I can just follow you, stay quietly out of the way. With the attacks that have happened so far, though, I don't feel right letting you be alone even in a school." More softly, Magnús added, "I want to keep you safe."

Altair looked torn. "If you're sure no one can see you, I guess it couldn't hurt. But *I* could see you." His facial expression showed doubt.

Magnús willed himself to fade from view. Altair blinked in surprise for a moment, and his eyes shifted around the car. Then he seemed to sharpen his gaze and stared into Magnús's eyes. "I admit that was weird, and you got fuzzy for a second, but you're right there."

It was unnerving, to say the least. Magnús had never been seen if he didn't wish to be visible. He concentrated harder, pulling more deliberately on his inherent magic to hide himself than he had in decades. Altair's eyes widened, and he looked around the cabin of the car.

"Wow, that's amazing. I can't see you at all now. No, wait... there's a kind of, uh, blur."

Magnús had to grit his teeth slightly to maintain his concentration, but he said, "You're something special, all right." Altair's cheeks reddened. "But even if you can see a hint of me, I'm sure no one else can."

Altair grumbled, but he got out of the car. He glanced up at the nearby statue, then did a double take. "Is that man beating a seal with a Bible?"

Magnús chuckled softly. "Sort of. That's a depiction of Sæmundur the Wise, reportedly the most learned human in Iceland. There are all kinds of stories about him, usually involving him outwitting the Devil. As I recall, this statue is based on a tale where Sæmundur tricked the Devil into turning into a seal to carry him to a job interview across the water."

"God, I love these legends," Altair murmured.

"Sæmundur promised his soul if the Devil could get him to

the shore without getting him wet. Just as they got across and it seemed the Devil would win, Sæmundur pulled out his Bible and hit the seal on the head. That made the Devil drop Sæmundur in the shallows, and so he lost the wager and Sæmundur's soul."

Altair grinned. Then he looked at the engineering building, and his smile faded.

"I'll just follow you inside," Magnús said quietly. He moved very close to Altair, so close he could brush a finger against Altair's jacket. Altair's breath stuttered briefly at the contact. "I'll stay right behind when you go through a door so no one notices me open it again. Just ignore me. When we're in a room, I'll move to a space out of the way, to keep an eye on things."

But he wouldn't move too far away. Altair was clearly a magnet for trouble. He'd apparently been swooped up by one or more people intent on manipulating him for nefarious ends, and damned if Magnús was going to let that continue.

Perhaps it was the threat to Iceland, or maybe it was just in the way Altair reminded him of Sigurjón, but Magnús would do everything in his power to keep this strange human safe from the forces of evil.

TWENTY-FIVE

Altair entered the building where he was to meet Professor Sigmundsdóttir and stared blankly at a directory written in Icelandic.

"It says her classroom is on the second floor," Magnús whispered in his ear. "That way."

Altair nodded and followed the invisible promptings. At the end of a hallway on the second floor, a large wooden door, inset with a window, seemed to be the classroom they wanted. Altair hesitated at the door, debating whether to knock, but a voice called out "Enter" before he could decide.

He pulled open the door and stepped into the room, aware from a quick press to his back that Magnús followed him in before the door swung closed again. Student desks similar to those in his own university were arranged in curving rows that descended, step by step, to a large, open area in which a bigger desk sat in a shaft of sunlight. A sturdy-looking woman with red hair, perhaps fifty years old, sat behind the desk, pen in hand, as she made some notes. Large windows behind her let in plentiful light, and a view of trees and a clear blue sky.

"Professor Sigmundsdóttir? I'm Altair Fálkason."

She nodded and rose, beckoning him to join her. "Welcome," the professor said, in accented English. "You are late, but allowances must be made, I suppose."

Altair squirmed slightly. Trusting Magnús to keep his word and stay at the back of the room, he walked down ten steps to shake the professor's firm hand.

She was about his own height and dressed in a gray suit with low-heeled black ankle boots. Hard blue eyes looked Altair up and down. For a moment, he thought her gaze flicked to look over his shoulder.

I'm just paranoid.

"Your mentor speaks highly of you, Mister Fálkason," she said, her slightly skeptical voice bringing heat to his cheeks.

"C-call me Altair. Please."

She sniffed. "How has your time in Iceland been so far?"

Screwy. Full of bad dreams and an insane swimming pool and cryptic elves. "Wonderful," Altair said, feeling formal and slightly awkward. "It's such a beautiful country."

"Indeed. You will soon see more of that which makes the land special. We have no time to dawdle. Come, let's review the plan."

She gestured him to the desk, where a map of Iceland lay open. Sticky notes attached to the map in certain locations coincided with the power plants Altair knew he was scheduled to visit. Some notations on the map itself in red pen, above the northern coast, drew his eye. They were in Icelandic so he couldn't read them, but it was puzzling. There was no power plant in that part of the country that he knew of.

"So," Professor Sigmundsdóttir began. "Today, we will go to the Hellisheiði Power Plant. It is an excellent location to survey the manner in which we use geothermal energy. Tell me what you know already of our systems."

"Oh. Well, the mantle plume underneath Iceland results in

groundwater that heats up as it flows through layers of rock. A series of boreholes bring the heated water to the surface."

"And then?" the professor prompted, moving around to the other side of the desk. She opened a drawer and pulled something out.

"I understand pipes bring the heated water directly to Reykjavik for all manner of public utilities. Heating of streets and homes, as well as hot water for consumption by the people for cooking and bathing."

"Yes, bathing. The waters of Iceland, heated by the fires banked deep beneath the surface over which humans sprawl." Professor Sigmundsdóttir met Altair's eye. "And, of course, warming their swimming pools...as your friend learned."

With a sound like a yowl, she threw the object in her hand right at Altair. It hit his chest with a splat. Tendrils or ropes slithered around his arms and legs. In a flash, he was tied up like a pole and fell over, hitting the classroom floor with a pained "oof."

Altair lay helpless on the ground, his arms and legs encased in something that felt vile. He heard Magnús's cry of alarm as Professor Sigmundsdóttir...changed. The woman's red hair thickened and grew coarser. It spread along her face and down her arms. Her legs and torso lengthened until she seemed six feet tall. Casually, she raked claws over her suit, shredding and tearing it away as she continued to grow. The grin she leveled over Altair's prone form—maybe Magnús had dropped his invisibility?—was full of too many sharp teeth.

Altair shivered in terror. What was happening? Who—or what—was this woman?

"The driver," she said, in a raspy voice that made Altair think of dead things. "We were suspicious when we heard that. Of course it's one of the huldufólk."

Magnús was behind Altair; twist as he might, Altair couldn't get himself around to see. To warn, or to, to... Well, shit. What would he do if he *could* see?

"Free him now, hag. I'm not going to tell you again." Magnús's voice was deep, steady, and even deadly. The menace in his tone! Altair hadn't known Magnús could sound like that.

Apparently, the professor wasn't impressed. She hissed a laugh through what were now clearly fangs. Her eyes had taken on slits, and her face, arms and legs were covered in thick orange fur. A thick tail lashed into view, and Altair could see her entire body was brindled in orange and brown fur.

"You're a cat!" he cried out. The thing that had been Ellen Sigmundsdóttir spared him a baleful glance. Suddenly, he felt very much like a trapped mouse and wished he hadn't reminded her of his presence.

"This could have been so much easier, if you'd just followed the itinerary. Ah well, I warned him you'd be found one way or another."

"Altair is under my protection," Magnús said, his voice closer now.

Ellen-the-cat rested her right foot, or paw, on Altair's throat. He cried out at a pinprick of claws pressing into his neck.

"Beware, elf," she said, with a laugh that curdled Altair's blood. "We don't need him able to talk. One more step and I'll rip his larynx to shreds."

After a short pause, Magnús said levelly, "He's a human, and he's not even from Iceland. Queen Hildur will not let this go. She will hunt you down and destroy you and your cohort. I will give you one. Last. Chance."

Altair barely restrained a gasp. A shimmer stepped up behind the cat-creature, the shape he knew to be an invisible Magnús. The creature seemed oblivious to Magnús's presence and kept its evil gaze on the place where Magnús's voice had come from.

The monstrous thing hissed. "Your queen loses her hold on

power day by day and doesn't even see it slipping away. Too long has she ignored the true people of this land. Her favoritism of the light elves, her willful ignorance of the creatures of land and sea, rock and tree, the nighttime wanderers—Yaowww!" she cried out as something struck the back of her head, knocking her away from Altair.

He yelped as her claws raked at his throat, but more in surprise than actual pain. Magnús became visible and dropped to the floor next to him.

"Are you all right?" The urgency and concern in his voice were so different from the menace he had leveled at the cat that Altair was momentarily stunned.

"I'm fine. Just scratched, I think."

Magnús nodded and stood, crouched, ready for a fight. Altair flinched and curled into himself as an orange blur flew at Magnús, carrying the elf back and out of sight. The sounds of a desk over-turning, of a baritone cry of pain, had Altair squirming to see what the hell was happening. Bound as he was, he wriggled and inched until his back met a riser in the floor. A feline snarl rent the air and turned to a deep, angry yowl just as he finally worked himself to a sitting position.

Magnús and the cat faced off in the area where the professor's desk now lay on its side. Magnús had a chair in one hand, its legs pointed at the beast. In the other, he held something that glowed blue. The cat-creature had grown even larger, until she was bigger than the tall elf. Her paws ended in scythe-like claws, and her teeth were like daggers. On her rear legs, tail lashing the air, she dodged Magnús's thrusts with the chair. A swipe of her forepaw knocked it out of Magnús's hand entirely.

"Look out," Altair cried uselessly as she sprang. Magnús made a desperate throwing motion with the glowing object—a stone, Altair thought—but the cat twisted its body, evading the missile. All of her weight landed on Magnús, claws sinking into his shoulders and belly. Magnús cried out in agony, and if a monster could grin, this one's face showed her delight at his pain.

"No!" Altair yelled. "Get away from him!"

The cat turned insolently toward Altair, fixing his gaze with her wicked eyes as she opened her jaw wide, wide, wider. Her pointed pink tongue curled as she turned back to contemplate the elf pinioned below her, and she lowered herself, almost crouching on top of Magnús. She was enjoying this, Altair realized, just like a regular cat with its prey.

Fury filled his body as he writhed and squirmed, desperate to stop the beast, stop this nightmare.

"Help!" he shouted. "Anyone. Bryndís. PLEASE!"

And *something* shifted inside him. He didn't know what it was, but the sound of his last cry echoed in the air of the classroom, not fading but growing louder.

The creature's enormous wildcat ears twitched and she looked at him again, slitted eyes narrowed. "What did you just do?"

Before Altair could answer, the glass windows at the end of the classroom exploded inward. A flock of gulls burst into the room, diving and pecking at the monster. She reared back, her claws pulling out of Magnús as she batted at the birds.

They were many, but the classroom was small and crowded. The birds were limited in what they could do, how they could maneuver. They struck and dove, drawing more hisses and angry yowls from the cat. Her wild sweeps knocked several birds out of the air, dashing them to the ground. The seagulls screamed and called, even as their numbers dwindled. In their battle cries, though, Altair thought he could make out a word.

"Mirror," Altair yelled to Magnús. "Trap her in a reflection. Something shiny or mirrored."

What the hell? He had no idea what he was saying, or why. Nor did Magnús, from the look on his face, but he pulled himself back from the melee between the cat and the remaining gulls.

Silvery liquid trailed behind him on the floor, leaving streaks. Was that what huldufólk had for—?

"Your blood!" Altair called. "Can you use that?"

Magnús rapidly whispered something like a chant, and a golden glow sprang to life inside his hands. The glow oozed to touch the closest shiny streak, and then the blood itself moved like mercury in a tube. It merged with another streak, then another, the liquid coming together to form a small, silvery pool that slid across the classroom floor to where the cat-creature fought and growled. Then the pool spread out, thinner and thinner, forming a disc at its feet.

Just as the cat-beast swiped the last of the gulls down, Magnús set off a flash of light that reflected in the silvery design, catching her attention. She hissed as her slitted eyes went to the reflective blood, but immediately she fell to all fours. Her tail went stiff but still, even as her eyes went wider, staring at the glimmering image on the floor, the mirror-like surface reflecting her monstrous face.

She stayed frozen, apparently unable to move. A low, menacing growl came from her throat, but she couldn't seem to pull her eyes away from the reflection of her own nature.

Magnús got painfully to his feet and limped to Altair. A swipe of his knife, and the bonds fell away. Altair's legs had already gone to sleep, Magnús was wounded and—from the mass of the silvery stuff he'd manipulated—had lost a lot of blood, so they leaned on each other as they ran the hell out of the classroom as fast as they possibly could.

CHAPTER

TWENTY-SIX

Sometime later, Altair slowly walked through the halls of the longhouse at the center of Hamarinn, trying to wrap his head around his life.

His scratches had somehow vanished during the drive to Hamarinn, but an elf with glowing hands had probed and touched him to make sure he wasn't harmed. She said she found nothing, though. Magnús had been taken somewhere to have his serious wounds treated, telling Altair they would meet later.

And so, Altair wandered and wondered, alone with his spiraling thoughts, in the strangest place he had ever seen. He had counted on Professor Sigmundsdóttir to explain the workings of geothermal power plants. Then the acclaimed academic he hoped might even become a mentor as he developed his dissertation...had turned out to be a cat. Or something cat-like.

She clearly intended to take Altair somewhere, to meet some mysterious "him," and she knew about the shit that went down at Sundhöllin. So was the cat-creature really Ellen Sigmundsdóttir? If not, then what had happened to the professor?

If Magnús knew what was going on, he wasn't saying. "To

185

protect me, my ass," Altair muttered. "You can protect me by telling me what the hell is going on."

He tried to distract himself by focusing on the beautiful longhouse. Its walls of smooth wood, lit by glowing stones instead of electricity or candles... That was something his brain could work on. What kind of energy was in use, and was it renewable? Could it be used for other purposes?

We were suspicious, the cat had said. Who was "we"?

This entire town defied his education and his understanding, with the cavern roof of apparently magical stones, with its farms and animals that thrived without benefit of sun. Perhaps a geothermal source was at work. His cell phone had been shattered in the fight, which really pissed him off because he had the strongest urge to get in touch with Willa or Professor Milton.

The sea gulls, my knowing Magnús could trap the cat-creature with its reflection.

Magnús was amazing to be around, but he ran hot and cold, soft and intense. Bryndís was out of a book of fairy tales. Diwata, Ólafur...both seemed like people Altair would hang out with to play video games, but one was a witch and one was an elf. As much as he was drawn to them all, he wasn't a part of their weird world. *His* world was an American town, an American university, American friends...

The word "we" crawled through his brain again, bringing a hint of nausea. The cat-creature had said "we were suspicious when we heard about the driver." Altair had only even mentioned that he had a driver to two people. And true, there was something a little odd about the way Willa and Jason were act—

He shuddered, cold fingers running down his spine as bees buzzed in his ears. The hallway seemed to spin for a second, disorienting him. No, there was no need to think that way, he decided. Willa and Jason were his friends. Professor Milton was his guide and mentor. The room in Boston was his safe place, his sanctuary.

The momentary dizziness eased, and Altair found himself walking down the hallway, trying to make sense of what his life had become.

Lady Bryndís came around a corner at that moment, in a slim-fitting but formal-looking robe. Her presence both soothed and alarmed him. She was so...regal.

"Good evening, Altair Fálkason. Thank you for our last meeting," she said, with a small bow to her head.

"Oh, um, you're welcome?"

The corners of Bryndís's lips turned up slightly. "You have had quite the adventure today. Are you well?"

Altair sighed. "To be honest, ma'am, I don't know."

"Please call me Bryndís." She extended a hand to rest on Altair's shoulder. "Come. Walk with me. Tell me how you are coping."

As they walked, Altair described what had happened that morning. "A woman who turned into an evil cat monster. I don't recognize my own life. I'm a student from Boston. I'm only in this country for a short time but I've got some creatures from fantasy trying to capture me, and others risking their lives to protect me."

Bryndís drew Altair's gaze to her own. "My son asked you before if you would like to leave Iceland, and you said no. With this latest attack, have you reconsidered?"

Hope leapt in Altair's chest. Could he leave now, today, knowing that something about his entire grant program was screwy? It was a perfect excuse, after all. How could Professor Milton and the others expect him to carry on as if his power plant tour was still a go, when his guide had turned out to be a were-cat?

But could he leave Magnús behind and never learn what it was in him that belonged in Iceland? More and more, he was feeling the pull of this strange country. The sense that something here wanted him, welcomed him, maybe even needed him...

"I-I don't know. I'm scared, but...yeah. I don't think I should leave, but what will happen if I stay?"

Bryndís didn't answer. Altair warred with his doubts silently, at one moment sure he should run, and the next picturing Magnús standing guard over his bound form, protecting him.

Eventually, Bryndís paused at a door. "And here we are. The room I wish to share with you."

The wooden door looked much like others in the longhouse, but Altair could feel something different about this one. A low hum vibrated in his skull, though he didn't think he was hearing it with his ears. He raised a hand to press against the wood; it was warm and almost pulsating. A throb started deep in his bones, and his belly seemed to flip. He moaned softly.

"What is it?" Bryndís asked, though he couldn't turn his head to see her. "What are you sensing?"

Dreamlike, he muttered, "Vastness. It's leading me to such empty space, where the wind brings me whispers. But it's not empty at all, is it? There are... are..."

"Worlds," Bryndís said in a low voice. "This room holds one of the roots of Yggdrasill the World Tree. The Nine Realms are there entwined in its branches. And you can somehow sense it even through an enchanted door." She paused, as if considering. "Do you wish to enter?"

Altair dropped his hand and stepped back, shaking his head. "I'm afraid of it," he whispered. "It's too much. If I go through that door—"

"I understand," Bryndís said kindly. "Your spirit knows what lies beyond, yet your body is not ready. Your heart is divided."

Altair looked up at her, feeling his eyes brim with tears. "I don't know what's happening to me. Do you know?"

She shook her head. "Forces are at work here beyond my ken, and I do not wish to press yet. Iceland is calling to you, Altair Fálkason, but for what purpose, the Nornir have not revealed.

Perhaps the land has a use for you, perhaps it is calling you home. And once you answer the call, your choices may narrow. I think your caution is wise."

"I can't stay here. My home is in Boston. My friends, my career," Altair said, almost desperately. His world should be in science and technology, not magic.

But an image of Magnús sprang to mind, a hand brushing back his long silver-blond hair, one of those slight grins on his lips. Was it foolish to imagine there could be anything between them?

"I can't stay, but I can't leave either," Altair amended hoarsely, hearing the strain in his own voice.

Bryndís was looking at him with a thoughtful expression. After a long moment, she said softly, "My son's fate is entwined with yours in a way we do not understand."

Altair opened his eyes wide. Did she know that he was thinking about Magnús? She promised not to read his mind, but... Oh god, his cheeks were burning.

Then her words registered. "Wh-what do you mean, our fates?" Altair asked.

But Bryndís shook her head. "I beg your indulgence, for I cannot explain at this time. You will know more once it is safe for you to know. For the moment, I will say only this. Some fears are wise, for they keep one alive. Other fears can keep one from living. True wisdom comes in understanding which fears must be faced and conquered."

"Um, okay."

"Come," Bryndís said decisively, resting a hand gently on Altair's shoulder. "If you are not ready to behold the World Tree, I will relate other tales of our land. You've encountered a ghoul cat, an urðarköttur. I will explain the magic that creates such a rare and dangerous beast while we return to the meeting hall."

CHAPTER
TWENTY-SEVEN

Magnús straightened in his chair when Altair entered the meeting chamber with Bryndís. He eagerly scanned Altair's face and throat to satisfy himself the wounds left by the urðarköttur had healed properly.

Altair's face lit up when their eyes met, and he hurried over to the table. "Are you all right?" he demanded, one hand outstretched to touch Magnús. But he yanked it back before he could make contact.

"I'm fine now. Our healer is strongly gifted. Your throat looks well, too." And despite himself, Magnús let his fingers reach up to trail lightly across Altair's unblemished neck. Altair flushed immediately but didn't pull away.

"A-*hem*," Diwata said noisily from her place across the table. "Two days, remember? There's time for all that later."

Altair turned his head to look at her, crooking it to one side. "Two days until what?"

"Never mind," Magnús and Ólafur said at almost the same time.

"You will know more—" Bryndís began.

"When it's safe for me, I know." Altair sighed. "Actually, I've been thinking about that as we walked. You say I zone out first, get all wonky. Right?"

"Yes," Magnús said cautiously. "You seem to lose a few moments of time and forget whatever has triggered the reaction."

"Now hear me out," Altair said. "There are warning signs, right?"

Ólafur's grin spread slowly. "Wait, are you going to propose we use you like a... what is the human simile?"

"A bird in a coal mine, I believe," Bryndís offered.

"A canary," Altair added, sounding resolute. "A canary in a coal mine."

"I don't know what a canary is doing in a coal mine," Magnús protested, "yet I have a feeling I'm not going to like this."

"You won't, but it's a great idea, if Altair is serious," Diwata said.

"My son, Altair proposes we talk—carefully—about our theories. If the sorcery works as we comprehend, he will exhibit symptoms as we get near to a truth."

"That's outrageous," Magnús exclaimed. "Altair, what if you sei—?"

"Careful, Cousin," Ólafur said, resting a hand on Magnús's arm. "This is a clever way to use the, um, enemy's magic against him. I can watch Altair's thoughts—with your permission, of course," he added with a nod to Altair, "while Diwata and Lady Bryndís guard against a magical attack."

"I need to do this," Altair said grimly before Magnús could voice more objections. "Whatever is happening is apparently pretty serious, and I don't like that I'm somehow a quest object in a game. So let's move this along to the boss fight."

"What?" Magnús asked weakly, deflating.

"Video game jargon," Ólafur said. "Don't worry about it.

Stick to your runestones." He winked at Altair, making the human smile.

All right, so Ólafur was helping Altair to relax, Diwata and Bryndís both thought this was a good idea, and Altair was on board. Magnús tried to find an objection anyway.

"It's not... The magic can run both ways..."

"I'm afraid, too, Magnús," Altair said. "But it's like your mother said to me a few minutes back. True wisdom comes in understanding which fears must be faced and conquered."

"A small test, first," Bryndís said, and gestured for Altair to take a seat. He pulled out a wooden chair next to Magnús and sat down.

Ólafur leaned close to Altair. "May I skim your mind? I promise I will not go any deeper than necessary to make sure you are safe." Altair swallowed hard, but he nodded jerkily.

Bryndís closed her eyes, and in moments a soft glow appeared around her. When she opened her eyes again, the blue in them appeared to dance. Altair gasped.

"Altair Fálkason, this is my place of power. I will use it all to keep you safe. I may have to put you to sleep, if you show signs of distress we cannot relieve."

Diwata had pulled some objects out of her satchel and arranged them on the table. "I'm preparing some magical wards as well. If anything gets through Lady Bryndís, I'll use galdur. Runic magic. You stay sharp, pretty boy," she said to Magnús, earning a grunt from Ólafur. "Keep your glow stones and knife ready, just in case. Okay, Altair. Ready?"

Altair nodded. "I'm ready. So, you all start talking about the verboten stuff, and I'll tell you if I feel strange."

Diwata took the lead. "So, I talked to those bastards at the witches council. They didn't want to help at first, but they could read the touch of the Nornir on me and voted to cooperate."

"And do they know of"— Bryndís paused, her glowing eyes turned to Altair —"a Black Priest?"

Altair's arm set up a tremor where it rested on the table.

"Nothing specific about a, uh, dark magician," Diwata said, pausing to see the effect. Altair's arm stilled, and his attention seemed present and focused. Ólafur nodded and mouthed all was well. "But they told me more about the Black School."

No reaction from Altair.

"Go on," Bryndís said. "As I recall, the human Sæmundur is involved in the story."

"Right. So, in the eleventh century, Sæmundur and two of his pals left Iceland and ended up in Paris. Or Oslo—those bozos on the council couldn't agree on just where the Black School was. Anyway, the guys were looking for food and a job, when an old man spoke to them in Icelandic. He invited them to study in his school, promised them shelter, and said when they left, they would be able to find the jobs of their dreams." Diwata grinned. "I think this is where the military got its game plan."

Bryndís tsked slightly. "The story, please."

"Okay, so the three amigos go in, get fed, and immediately they're put to work studying these books of magic. There are other men studying, too, but no one will speak to them. They begin to understand that they are reading books of black magic—"

"Altair!" Magnús cried. The trembling had returned over his whole body now. Bryndís stretched across the table to rest a glowing hand on Altair's, and immediately he calmed.

Looking around dazedly, Altair said, "I'm sorry, I think I dozed off for a moment. Were you talking to me?"

"It is quite all right," Bryndís said. "You are doing so well."

Diwata was scribbling in a notebook she'd pulled from her bag. "Got it, hot topic. Okay. So. They learn that they've entered the Black School, and dude at the door is actually the Devil.

"Well, Sæmundur immediately asks around about how they

get the fuck—sorry, Lady Bryndís—the heck out of there. There's only one way. Once a year, the Devil takes the students who have mastered the, um, work to a staircase. They can all run up, but the Devil will take the hindmost. The ones who make it can go out into the world and spread the evil they've learned. The loser spends the rest of existence as the Devil's lapdog or handmaid or something."

Altair had leaned in to listen, elbows on the table, looking fascinated. Magnús couldn't help a swell of fondness and pride. Their eyes met, and Altair's cheeks reddened. But he smiled at Magnús.

Diwata was still talking. "Years go by and finally the three friends are ready to graduate. One is kinda heavy, the other has a bad foot, so they figure ol' Sæmundur will be safe. But Sæmundur has been thinking about this for years, and he gets a clue. He uses the shi—uh, the stuff they've learned, and he enchants a dagger. He tells his friends to run as hard as they can, and he will go slower so they can get out. Blah blah blah, he's so noble, everyone tells him to get free, but his mind's made up.

"The Devil herds the graduating class together at a closed door. He gestures, and they suddenly get that they've been in Hell the whole time they were studying."

"Humans have a different concept of Hell than we do," Magnús offered to Ólafur, who looked confused. "It's a bad place, like Svartálfaheimur, instead of the land where the goddess Hel rules."

"Our dark elf kin in Svartálfaheimur are not bad," Bryndís commented reprovingly. "They have their own ways."

"Can I finish my story?" Diwata asked. "Okay, when the Devil drops the flag, the graduates all start to run, pushing and shoving each other back to try to get out. Sure enough, Sæmundur's friends are slow, but he deliberately goes even slower, urging them up. The Devil's hopping back and forth from one hoof to the other at the bottom of the staircase, loving the fun. The staircase climbs higher and higher, they've been panting and struggling up for what seems like an hour, and then the Devil gives a whoop and begins to run up the stairs after them.

"Well, Sæmundur whispers a spell he picked up, and his shadow gets thicker and solid. It looks just like Sæmundur, but it's still his shadow, so it's attached. His friends are almost at the top, he's right behind them, when the Devil gets there and grabs. But what he gets hold of is the shadow.

"He shouts in triumph, holding on to the fake and cackling. Before he can figure out he's been tricked, Sæmundur whips out his enchanted knife and slices right through the foot of the shadow, where it's attached to him. The shadow-Sæmundur comes loose in the Devil's arms. He stumbles and falls back down the steps, still holding on to the shadow, while Sæmundur and all his buds escape through the top!" Diwata finished with a flourish.

Altair clapped his hands. "I love that story. Hey, wait," he said to Magnús. "Wasn't there a statue of Sæmundur at the University of Iceland?"

Magnús nodded. "Yes, he appears in quite a few stories after this one. Most are about the Devil trying to get him, and Sæmundur outsmarting him."

"Weird that there are these Christian legends and ideas mixed in with Norse legends," Altair said. "You don't have a devil in your mythology, do you?"

"Child, what you call myth is our reality," Bryndís said. "I have never met Jesus or any of the saints or demons the human religions here preach, but I have met and spent time with the Æsir and the Vanir. The Nornir sent us to you."

Altair blushed. "I'm sorry, I didn't mean to be rude. It's just, in the States, we learn about the Norse myths like something old and forgotten, same as Greek and Roman."

"The gods are not forgotten here," Bryndís said. "We revere

and welcome them. Whether the Christian god or his angels visit, I could not say."

"Do you have a Devil?" Altair asked. "I mean, in your religion or your worship?"

"Not as the human religion has it," Magnús said. "Surtur is the lord of the fire giants of Muspellsheimur. He is probably the basis for some of the popular western images of Satan. Dante, for example, described Satan in the Inferno as a giant with wings, trapped in ice. Your country often pictures Hell as a place of fire, with fiery demons torturing the souls of the damned."

Ólafur tilted his head. "Come to think of it, the fire giant we saw in the vision—"

"Careful!" Diwata shouted, but it was too late. Altair shivered and sagged, his eyes going vacant. Bryndís uttered a word as the glow from her hand spread to Altair, and he closed his eyes. His trembling eased at once.

When he opened his eyes again, a few moments later, they were clear.

"What just happened?" Magnús demanded.

"Altair experienced a loud buzzing, and his mind clouded," Ólafur explained. "Bryndís's magic soothed him, and it's gone now. Altair, I beg your pardon for my carelessness."

"Um, no problem? Did you learn anything by...whatever that was?"

"Yes," Magnús answered, lightly brushing a hand over Altair's. "You gave us an important clue. Thank you."

Altair beamed at him. "Keep going, then."

Bryndís said, "Did you notice that the story of the knife produced no response, but the work at the institution and the image of, well, *that* did trouble Altair?"

"So the knife isn't relevant to whatever is happening?" Ólafur asked.

"I am not certain of that," Bryndís replied. "The tale resonates with me, and I recall others about Sæmundur's dagger. Perhaps our enemy simply is unaware of it."

"Maybe." Diwata shrugged. "I was thinking about the other students, the ones who ran up the stairs ahead of Sæmundur and his friends. They left the Black School to go out into the world. Someone like that might be considered a...you know." She folded her hands as if in prayer.

"I agree about the religious connection," Bryndís said. "Recall as well the books the students were studying. In searching through my memories, I revisited a certain Gottskálk grimmi Nikulásson who died perhaps five hundred years ago." Eyes fixed on Altair, she said slowly, "He was a high officiant in the church—"

Altair swallowed hard. "Something...uh, I feel something. But keep going."

"His diocese was in Hólar in the north. This...*figure* was notorious for his cruelty, hence the name grimmi. And as Diwata has reminded us, he was the author or at least owner of a galdrabók..."

She paused, and Altair, trembling, nodded at her. His lips were tight, but he got out, "Go on. But it's rising."

"Hólar..." Magnús squeezed his eyes, trying to place the name. "When I arrested Vörður, he was there. I never found out why."

Ólafur leaned closer to Altair, grim-faced. "I can feel something stirring as well. Let me try..." He closed his eyes in concentration.

Magnús was torn between the desire to stop what was happening and the awareness they were onto something crucial. He reached for Altair's hand. "Shall we stop?"

Altair shook his head tightly even as he squeezed Magnús's hand.

"All right." Magnús looked back to Bryndís, who also sat rigidly, prepared to act, the glow in her eyes even brighter now.

"I will not name the book," she said, "but after this man died, it disappeared. Many sorcerers attempted to recover it. One even recalled the spirit of Gottskálk to force the location from him but failed."

"I know legends of...that book," Diwata said. "Very dark stuff. Spells to call killing storms. To force transformations. To enslave—"

Altair kicked away from the table violently, his chair falling backwards so he hit his head on the stone. Bryndís reached Altair at the same moment as Magnús, placing her hands on his head and commanding him to sleep.

Magnús gently repositioned Altair so the human's head was in his lap. The sleep spell seemed to work, because his body was quiet again.

"I'm helping him dream of other things," Ólafur said behind them. "His mind is calm. Whatever was alerted as we talked...I can't sense it in him now. But it felt strongly like a separate presence, pushing back against something within Altair."

"We need to find a way to break his enchantments," Magnús said, stroking Altair's hair from his eyes. "I hate the toll this takes. It isn't right that Altair assumes risks when he doesn't understand how bad it has already been for him, before."

"Altair Fálkason is brave, my son. Do not doubt his courage nor discount his willingness to fight."

"I'm not," Magnús protested. "I see that he's strong. But he has no experience of our world and our dangers."

"Yet through his courage, he has given us significant guidance," Bryndís said. "Although I would not have uttered the word while Altair was awake, Gottskálk was a bishop of the humans' Christian church. And another word for a spell that enslaves is..."

Magnús inhaled sharply. "A shackle."

TWENTY-EIGHT

Magnús strode away from the longhouse, under the rippling light of Hamarinn, and toward the farm of his uncle, Berkir. He'd left Altair, with some trepidation, in the care of Bryndís. The gods send that she didn't traumatize him with her intensity.

The conversation had reminded him of the oddness of having arrested his cousin Vörður in Hólar. At the time, he'd wondered why Vörður was there. The town was near Akureyri, itself the largest collection of humans in Iceland outside of Reykjavik, but Hólar was not one huldufólk tended to frequent.

After the discussion of an evil bishop from the same town, Magnús knew he needed to find out more.

Vörður, fortunately, was magically compelled to remain in his father Berkir's house and so was nearby. Berkir's fields, thanks to Ólafur's tending, were lush, some crops probably nearing harvest. The scent of ripening tomatoes and peppers tickled his nose as he neared Berkir's farmhouse. A green smell of kale and cabbage mingled with the animal smells of the farm's livestock. From a penned area of sheep and lamb drifted low bleats and the odor of wet wool.

Familiarity brought an involuntary smile to Magnús's face. He'd never been much interested in the agrarian life growing up, but Ólafur had been his closest companion as a young elf. Since Ólafur had always loved the fields and animal husbandry that still made up a big part of life for the huldufólk, Magnús had some-times found himself with a pitchfork in hand, or ankle-deep in manure, to help.

Ólafur had been so excited when he learned how humans used the bountiful geothermal energy of Iceland to power hot houses in which they could grow exotic and foreign crops like tomatoes. The warmth of Hamarinn had served the same purpose, once he witnessed the example of human farms. The novelty of the things Ólafur grew was the reason Berkir's farm was among the most successful among the huldufólk.

Thoughts of Ólafur tending his own family's crops and studying human technology gave way to an idle thought: *Altair would be fascinated by comparing human engineering to huldufólk magic.*

Magnús could almost picture the delight on Altair's expressive, unguarded face as he entered a greenhouse. In his mind's eye, they approached a hot house early in the morning, under a dark sky, so that, through panes of glass, the structure glowed like a yellow diamond. Inside, the sweet tang of basil, the buzzing of bees imported to pollinate the crops, the brilliance of red tomatoes climbing vertical racks the humans used to maximize their growing space, would bring Altair to an open-mouthed halt. Magnús could see it so clearly, and he wanted to be the one to show it all to the young human.

A sudden stab of guilt wiped the smile from Magnús's face. Sigurjón would also have loved to see what innovations the humans had made since his years. Even if time and natural death would have prevented it, still, there was much he and Magnús could have shared. *Should* have shared.

The reminder of Sigurjón steeled him for his purpose. As he reached the farmhouse, he called out a mental greeting.

«Berkir Mother's-brother, may I enter?»

Berkir stepped out of the door, a pewter mug in one hand. Much like Ólafur, Berkir dressed in loose linen shirts and casual brown trousers suited to field work. His resemblance to Bryndís was clear, but where her gaze was cool and proud, Berkir's stormy blue eyes narrowed at Magnús. His cheeks flushed.

Rather than answer in mind-speech, Berkir all but growled, "Are you here to cause more trouble for my children, Magnús Sister-son? Is it Óli you now think to plague?"

Magnús bit down the sharp words of self-defense and of attack that sprang to his tongue. With thoughts of Sigurjón fresh to mind, he wanted to say that, if Berkir's children Lars and Vörður had learned at home to value humans more...

But no, that would avail him nothing, only alienate Berkir further. He bowed his head respectfully and answered, "Uncle, I grieve that my duty has created a division between us. Nevertheless, I ask your permission to enter and to speak with Vörður, if he will allow it."

Berkir grunted and took a sip from his mug. After a lengthy pause, he turned his head toward the house.

Magnús could hear a whisper of his uncle's query. «That self-righteous sister-son wants to talk to you, do you want to talk to him?»

Given Magnús's well-known limitations with mind-speech, Berkir almost certainly shared the insulting thoughts deliberately. Another moment passed, then Berkir sighed.

"All right. Vörður will speak with you. I am not best pleased to welcome you into my house, Magnús, but since the enchantment imposed upon my son keeps him confined to the interior, you may enter."

Berkir moved out of the doorway. With another tight bow, Magnús stepped past him and into the dwelling. He made his way deeper into the interior and stopped at a closed door he knew well, from when he and Ólafur had been all but inseparable and spent hours in the house.

At a knock, Magnús received a drawled, "Enter, jailer."

So that was how this encounter would go. Fine. Magnús set his jaw and opened the door.

Vörður lay sprawled across a chair, long legs dangling, a book in one hand. He looked like Ólafur except for his dark red hair.

"How are you, Vörður?" Magnús tried politely.

"Bored. Trapped. Horny," Vörður bit out. "Can you help with any of those things, Cousin? Oh wait, you're the one who put me here."

"I'm the one who saved you, Cousin," Magnús snapped.

Vörður's eyes flashed, though he kept to a slow drawl. "How do you figure that bit of self-righteousness?"

"If you had actually succeeded in switching yourself for that American family's baby and left the country, the queen would have ordered your execution as a changeling. As it is, I got the real baby back from the gnomes and hauled your ass out of there. You're welcome."

Vörður slammed his book to the ground and leapt up from the chair, indolent act dropped. "Hildur would have had to find me first. And she's about to be so busy I would have had plenty of time to lose myself in the United States."

"Why is *Queen* Hildur about to be busy?"

Vörður barked a laugh. "So. The self-appointed sheriff has no idea of the game afoot? The champion of humans and their filthy cities and boringly short lives has no clue that he's soon to be out of a job?"

"What's about to happen? Dammit, Vörður. Don't make your situation worse. If you know something important—"

"Worse?" Vörður interrupted, his features red now. "Worse? You fool. You have no idea how bad things are going to get. You want to know why I replaced that mewling infant? Because I want out of Iceland before it all goes to what the Christians call Hell. Literally, to their Hell."

"Then tell me what's going on, Cousin. Let me try to stop it, or at least give me something to bring to... Wait. Hold on. Does it have anything to do with this symbol?" Magnús sketched a sigil in the air, the rune he'd seen in three places.

Vörður looked startled for a moment, then he sighed deeply. His shoulders sagged. "Well. You aren't so stupid after all." He waved his hand, dissipating the traces of magic Magnús had left in the air. His eyes darted to the door of his room and the house beyond. "I'll tell you something because we're cousins. Don't do that again where the wrong people might see."

"Berkir?" An almost imperceptible shake of Vörður's head, and then Magnús got it. "Lars. What is that son of a bitch up to?"

Vörður hesitated, seemed about to speak, but then he drew himself to his full height. "You're the reason I'm here instead of in a penthouse apartment in New York City, with a nanny and a new world to explore. Quid pro quo. You get the queen to lift the enchantment that keeps me in Berkir's farmhouse and unable to use my shape-changing magic, and I'll tell you what I know."

Magnús growled. "I'd need more than your vague warnings to get anywhere with Queen Hildur."

"Then go to the trolls, Cousin. Go to Grýla the Trollmother. She's not happy about the situation either. She's smart for a troll, though she doesn't truly understand what's at stake. But you should be able to get enough out of her to persuade the queen to make a deal with me. Once I'm guaranteed a way out of this place, I'll tell you what is coming."

TWENTY-NINE

A few hours later, Magnús said from behind the wheel, "You don't have to come with us."

Altair was in the passenger seat beside him, while Diwata and Ólafur sat on either side of a small table built into the floor of the van.

Diwata scoffed. "You may be 'Magnús of the Hidden Ways,' but I'm the one the Nornir spoke to. I'm part of this, too."

"We're all involved in one way or another, Cousin," Óli said. "This is right, that we accompany you. I feel it."

"Fine." Magnús concentrated on the road ahead.

After returning the borrowed Renault, he'd liberated a camper van from an agency that rented them to tourists and vacationing families. Magnús's gift told him to seek Grýla in the lava fields near Lake Mývatn. The fields were only about a seven-hour drive on the Ring Road that encircled Iceland. They'd gotten a late start, what with locating a proper van and making plans with Bryndís, but he hoped they'd be near Grýla's cave by three or four in the morning.

He had considered opening the Hidden Ways to get them to

the area where Grýla made her lair, but the magic took so much out of him that he worried he wouldn't have enough left to protect Altair if things turned ugly.

And with a troll, things were likely to turn ugly.

Altair's eyes were glued to the rock formations interspersed with homes and businesses as the van headed north from Reykjavik. Soon, the buildings grew sparse, and the landscape revealed itself. Bronze-colored fields spread on either side of the highway, their tundra cover looking soft as velvet. In one direction, the afternoon sun glittered like diamonds on the water of an icy-blue fjord. In another, red-roofed farm buildings stood in sharp relief against stark black hills.

Magnús found himself darting glances at Altair, who stared out through the passenger-side window, fingertips on the glass. For reasons that were unclear to him, Magnús very much wanted Altair to appreciate the beauty out there. He resisted the temptation to peek into Altair's mind, though.

The speakers in the van blared with so-called music (Magnús reserved judgment) from a group called Zhrine. Diwata insisted they had to hear the band's "doom metal" on their road trip.

"You're gonna love this song," she said to Ólafur. "It's 'Spewing Gloom.'"

Magnús was almost sure that was a joke at his expense. But as Diwata had brought more of her freshly baked breads, he decided he could ignore it.

Altair seemed as much in love with Diwata's baking as he was, from the way he tore into a cinnamon roll covered in thick pink icing that tasted slightly of black currant. The treats consumed, silence stretched between them. But it wasn't long before Magnús drove them into the tunnel that stretched beneath Hvalfjörður. He wasn't at all surprised when Altair began to pepper him with questions he couldn't answer.

"How old is this tunnel? How did they build it, under the

fjord? How is it protected from earthquakes? From volcanic eruptions?"

"You're an engineer. You probably know more about this than an ancient elf."

Altair snorted. "I already agreed you aren't ancient. And you're right, I took some relevant courses, but I went in a different direction before I studied how to nature-proof a structure in an area with so much seismic activity." He sighed. "I was hoping to learn specifically about that when Professor Sigmundsdóttir took me to the different power plants."

Altair looked out the window again as they emerged from the tunnel, silent and thoughtful.

Diwata and Ólafur talked animatedly behind them, about their favorite bands, the latest video game.... Magnús worried they didn't take the risks seriously.

Altair's face continued to alternate between wonder and consternation as the van drove north. He remained silent, though, for a surprisingly long time. While Diwata and Ólafur debated the perfect road song, Magnús quietly prodded Altair, "What are you thinking?"

Altair sighed deeply. "Today, I was supposed to be touring a power plant at Egilsstaðir. Writing notes for my dissertation. Instead, I'm driving along fjords and mountains with two elves and a witch, to escape a were-cat and maybe other shit trying to hurt us. Magic instead of science. I don't understand any of this."

"I'll explain as soon as I can," Magnús said, once again. "We're safe in here. Diwata bespelled the van to make sure our location cannot be scried. The huldufólk and other inhabitants rarely think about using something so human as a vehicle and a highway."

Suddenly, Diwata cut off her music and grasped Magnús's shoulder. "Can we detour into Borgarnes? I just remembered that my friend Yrja lives there. She's one of the few women witches, and she helped teach me when none of the men would.

She might have some insight the witches council 'forgot' to share."

Magnús agreed a short delay wouldn't affect their plans much, so he exited the Ring Road and let his gift guide them to Yrja.

As they navigated the narrow city streets of the ancient town, Ólafur leaned forward between the front seats to look out the front windshield. "We're near the grave of Skalla-Grímur Kveldúlfsson, aren't we? Dee, remember when we went to that festival there?"

"With all the rock inspired by the Sagas?" Diwata replied with glee. "Of course! That was insane. Yrja has a store not far from there, and she's leery of huldufólk. Why don't you drop me off, show Altair the thing, and I'll meet you after I talk to Yrja?"

"Okay," Altair said skeptically as he, Magnús, and Ólafur got out of the van to look at the cairn of rust-colored rocks, bound with a heavy chain. "Who is Skalla-Grímur?"

"Just a berserker son of a werewolf who tried to kill his son Egil a few times," Magnús said, stretching himself from side to side.

Ólafur looked over the plaque near the burial mound. "I have to admit that the sagas the humans tell of their experience here in Iceland fascinate me. Egil's Saga is my favorite."

"Egil is some kind of Icelandic hero?" Altair asked.

"Not exactly," Ólafur said thoughtfully. "He was a long-lived man who did many important things, in human terms, but he did a lot of bad things too. He composed his first poem when he was three, killed a playmate when he was seven. You know." He winked at Altair. "A typical human boy."

"Hæ, Magnús! What are you doing here?"

Magnús whirled around at the sound of Karl's voice. His friend, clad in a red and blue Search and Rescue jacket against the chilly air, hurried toward them down the sidewalk. They clasped forearms.

"It's good to run into you," Magnús said. "Karl, may I present my friend Altair Fálkason and my cousin Ólafur Berkisson."

Karl shook with each of the other men, grasping the outstretched hand of Ólafur first, then taking Altair's hand in both of his.

"It's nice to meet you, Altair. My name is Karl Bjarnason. I work with Magnús from time to time on, er, odd business."

"Hello. Magnús, is this the guy you said might help you with that symbol from my hotel?"

Magnús slapped his forehead. "I forgot about that. Thank you, Altair."

He fumbled in his pocket and produced the sketch Diwata had shared with him. "Do you recognize this, Karl?" He explained about seeing it on the troll cave and Altair's hotel, though he didn't dare mention it was also branded on Altair's throat.

Karl studied the sketch. "I did see this before, but I didn't know it was important." He pulled out his smartphone and scrolled through pictures. "Yes. Here."

Magnús looked over Karl's shoulder at the image of another troll disaster. The picture revealed a mangled campsite. A piece of cloth was draped over what looked like a ripped-apart backpack. Karl used two fingers to enlarge the photo so Magnús could see the same mysterious symbol was painted onto the cloth.

"Where was this?" Magnús asked.

"Up near Akureyri," Karl said. "Some colleagues investigating a disappearance sent the pictures. We weren't positive trolls were involved, but with this symbol..."

"It certainly fits," Magnús agreed. "What next?"

"Well," Karl drawled, scratching his beard, "I think I need to go join the search for those campers, now that we pretty much can confirm troll involvement."

Magnús began to protest that tackling trolls was too dangerous, but Altair's gasp distracted him.

"Trolls? You think *trolls* are kidnapping people?" Altair demanded. "Wait, don't tell me. You can't explain for my own good."

Ólafur threw an arm around Altair's neck. "I don't care what Lars says, you humans can be pretty smart sometimes." He grimaced at the dark look Magnús knew he was showing. "Okay, bad joke. But, Altair, you know we're just looking out for you."

"I guess, but man, it sucks being in the dark like this."

Diwata joined them then. "Hæ, Kalli. How's Bjarni?" she asked, throwing her arms around his waist.

"Cantankerous," Karl said. He sniffed at Diwata's hair. "You smell of pine, birch, and citrus. I'm guessing you've just come from Yrja's store."

"You think she'd be willing to help one of the few other female witches, but she's as stubborn as the pigs on the witches council. She did lend me this, though." Diwata held out a polished piece of green stone with a rune engraved on it. "It's a way finder. It warms when I'm getting near to something I want to see or find, but I have to be fairly close already before it works. Yrja says mostly it just helps with the last thousand yards or so if she's looking for herbs or something. It led me to you just now."

She wrapped the stone in a piece of silk and put it in her pouch. "What are you doing here in Borgarnes?" she asked Karl.

When he'd explained again, Diwata pulled a piece of charcoal from her pouch, grabbed Karl's left hand, and sketched a rune that Magnús thought looked dwarvish.

"It's a rune of protection against rock falls," she explained. "It might do some good against a troll. Just don't wash that hand until you're safe again."

Karl looked at the rune and chuckled. "Well, I'll do my best to keep it—and me—safe." He bowed formally. "Thank you, Witch Pétursdóttir."

Ólafur was watching the exchange between Karl and Diwata

with a slight frown. Magnús stepped next to him and nudged him with an elbow.

«They're just friends. Both connected to witch culture. It's natural for friends to look out for each other.»

«Friends that are both human and live in a human world,» Ólafur sent back grumpily. «Plus, this Karl guy is handsome, and he has the whole search-and-rescue hero vibe going on.»

Handsome? Magnús looked again at Karl. Not a word he would use for the thickly built, fiercely bearded man, but to each his own. He reached out to grasp Karl's shoulder. "Don't take any risks. Trolls are too dangerous to tackle without magic."

Karl grunted. "It isn't your job to keep everyone safe, Magnús. I and my team are trained professionals. We go into dangerous situations all the time. Trust us to apply caution, but if we can save missing people, we will."

With that, Karl returned to his own task, and the rest of them climbed back into the camper. As they resumed their journey, Ólafur distracted Altair with a summary of Egil's Saga, provoking gasps and laughter at appropriate points in the story.

Diwata said, "The one I always liked in school was Eyrbyggja Saga. Remember the bit about Oddur and his mother Katla the witch? Katla cast a bunch of spells so the men hunting Oddur couldn't see him. Another witch hated her and helped the men who were after Oddur. The second witch threw a sealskin bag over Katla's head, and that stopped Katla from casting any more spells."

"And this is what you study in school?" Altair asked. "That's way more fun than the stuff I remember reading."

CHAPTER

THIRTY

Magnús drove north but studied Altair surreptitiously while he talked with Diwata and Ólafur. Altair loved the stories, Magnús had realized already. He was fascinated by the lore of Iceland, even though his training made him doubtful. Well, the experiences he was undergoing should certainly open up his mind.

Eventually, quiet reigned as they continued the drive along the Ring Road. Its stark, winding line of black cut across wide, flat fields of bronze grass that were just starting to turn green. The occasional flocks of sheep, with little white lambs bouncing along besides ewes, had Altair wide-eyed in delight. A stream splashing along a rocky bed, casting up mist and a rainbow in the evening sun, made him gasp.

And then a small herd of Icelandic horses had Altair insisting they stop the camper. His gaze roamed over the sturdy beasts, with their chestnut or gray or roan double coats and long manes rippling in the wind.

"They're short compared to horses I saw in the States," Altair said, his longing clear. "I always wanted to learn to ride, but none of the foster families I was placed with did stuff like that."

Ólafur and Magnús exchanged a glance, then Óli said, "I raise a few horses on my family farm in Hamarinn. When we get back, I can teach you how to ride."

Altair turned shining eyes on Ólafur, with a grateful look that suddenly gave Magnús a pang of jealousy. "That would be amazing. These seem like the right size for a shrimp like me."

"Icelandic horses are strong and sturdy," Ólafur said. "They were originally brought over from Norway by the human settlers in the ninth century. No other horses can be imported here, and if one of these horses leaves the country, it can never return for fear of introducing a disease."

He continued telling Altair about the special fauna of Iceland as they drove on. Winds buffeted the camper from time to time, especially as they crossed large, open expanses of meadow. Altair then began explaining to Ólafur how wind turbines worked, his gestures becoming more animated as his passion overcame his shyness and uncertainty. Magnús listened closely, intrigued at the way humans used engineering to accomplish things his race did with magic.

They had been on the road for several hours more when Diwata groaned. "I suppose you huldufólk can go forever without sleep, but I'm exhausted. It's past eleven already, and we have another three hours to go. I'll be useless if I don't get some sleep, and I bet the same is true for Altair."

Mindful of the warning from the Nornir about the new moon, Magnús wanted to press on. But it was safer to approach Grýla in the daytime, when they were rested and could escape her cavern into the sun if needed. He couldn't help grumbling, though. "All right, watch for a place to turn off the road."

Soon enough, they located a small side road that led into a grove of trees, where a campsite had been established for travelers.

The grove bordered a pond that seemed fed by a fjord beyond. No other camper vans were in sight when Magnús parked.

The vehicle they'd borrowed had two berths and also a roof tent that could be set up on top of the van. Magnús studied the tent contraption built onto the roof but could make no sense of it.

Ólafur stood next to him, looking up at the aluminum and canvas. He shrugged. "Maybe it will be easier to sleep on the ground."

"I got this," Altair said. Deftly, he drew out some struts that Magnús hadn't even realized were part of the equipment, set them into the ground as a ladder, then climbed up to unfold the canvas tent.

"Pretty efficient design," Altair said, his voice muffled by the material as he worked. "Lightweight, easy to erect and to stow…"

Ólafur shook his head at Magnús, bemused. "Humans," he said and shrugged. "I'll make a fire if you want to protect the site."

Diwata sat on a wooden bench nearby, a map open before her and a small witch-light drifting above the table. She glanced at Magnús. "Do you want me to add some wards?"

"Possibly. I'll position my runestones, and you can add anything you feel appropriate."

Altair joined them. "The tent is up and secure. What can I do to help?"

"There's a bag of food Bryndís sent with us," Magnús said. "Perhaps you could set that out for our supper."

Altair grinned up at him, saluted, and sauntered off to obey.

Magnús shook his head in bemusement. He regretted again the lies and half-truths they had to tell to keep Altair's enchantment from triggering and possibly killing him. While Magnús moved around the campsite setting up a perimeter, he couldn't help but reflect on the two humans he had led into peril.

Sigurjón might have lived longer if I'd trusted him with more truths. The voice in his head was full of self-loathing. If Magnús had warned Sigurjón more about the dangers of associating with the huldufólk, or if he had stayed away from him entirely, the young man might have had a full and rich life. Magnús had made an enemy of Lars when they were young, and Lars had turned their private feud into an excuse for murder.

And now, Lars was back from exile to work more mischief. Vörður had said as much. Somehow, it related to the prophecy of Altair's danger.

Aloud, Magnús muttered, "What is that bastard up to now? He's planning something, I'm sure of it."

THIRTY-ONE

Altair avidly watched Ólafur work a spell to light a campfire. "So cool. But is a fire a good idea?"

Ólafur shrugged. "There are generally a lot of humans camping throughout the countryside. I don't think one more fire will draw unusual attention."

Altair heard Magnús growl then, about a "bastard." Pretty clear who Magnús meant. "Wow, this Lars guy really bothers Magnús, huh?"

"You could say that." Ólafur sighed.

"I think I heard Lars was related to you?"

"He's my brother. I once worshipped the ground he walked on, until his dislike of humans became fanaticism. I love humans, but I love Lars, too, even if I cannot abide his actions. If he is indeed part of this mess, I hope I can persuade him of his errors before something terrible and irreversible happens."

"Wow, that's, uh, really tough. I'm sorry, Óli. What did Lars do to piss Magnús off?"

"Magnús should be the one to explain. Has he told you anything?"

"Just that Lars did something bad to a human that got him exiled from Iceland for a while."

"Seventy-five years." Ólafur sighed. "No one was happy about that."

"What do you mean?"

"Magnús wanted Lars punished more harshly. The rest of my family thought the exile was too harsh. You can't imagine what it means for the huldufólk to be cut off from our home. The light of Álfheimur...well, it flows weakly in the rest of Miðgarður, I've been told."

"You mean the Earth, right?" Altair paused, then asked carefully, "And how did you feel about Lars's punishment?"

Ólafur looked up at him from where he crouched. Silence stretched as he seemed to weigh his words. At last, he said simply, "Lars is my brother. And he was wrong. But I don't know that the exile did anything to show him that."

THEY SAT around the picnic table a little later, with a few floating lights that Diwata had conjured drifting around like oversized fireflies. Above them, the sky was still royal blue, despite the late hour. A barely there sliver of moon shone through the sparse tree branches.

The provisions Bryndís had arranged for them were delicious. Diwata also produced some rye rolls, so good they had Altair moaning. Despite the seriousness of the situation, he chuckled.

"I'm eating food provided by elves and a witch. This won't put me to sleep for a century, will it?"

The others didn't get the reference, so Altair told the story of Rip Van Winkle. Ólafur countered with an Icelandic tale of two troll sisters who kidnapped a prince and put him in an enchanted sleep every day until they could force him to marry one of them.

Later, after clearing up, Altair said to Magnús, "I was useless when we were attacked before. Do you think you could teach me some defensive moves?"

Magnús considered. "Well, I see no harm in starting. Here, get to your feet."

After that, Magnús gave Altair some training in how to duck and roll out of the way if they were ever in a fight. It was harder than Altair had suspected, and he broke a sweat quickly. The night wasn't especially cold—or he was growing use to Iceland's weather—so he wore only his sweater as he rolled in the dirt of the campsite. Being in motion helped distract him, though. Iceland, Boston, Magnús, magic...he welcomed the respite from his swirling thoughts.

When Magnús said they'd done enough for one night, Altair went to the pond to wash his face and hands. By the time he came back, Diwata was calling an end to the evening.

"We've got a lot to deal with tomorrow. Let's get as much sleep as we can."

Magnús said, "I'll take the first watch."

With that, Diwata gave Ólafur a little smile, rose from the table, and climbed into the camper to claim one of the beds. Ólafur froze, looking discomfited. Magnús bumped his arm. "You might as well take the other bunk in there, Cousin. Altair and I will use the tent."

"I'll take second watch," Ólafur said as he rose to follow Diwata.

"Why don't I do that?" Altair said, with a wink to Magnús. "You probably need your sleep."

Ólafur nodded but didn't respond, his eyes fixed on the camper door.

When he'd climbed in, Altair leaned close to Magnús. "What's the story there?"

"I don't know for certain, but my cousin seems quite taken with Diwata."

"She's a spitfire. I like her."

"I...am growing to as well. You should get in the tent, so you can rest. Elves don't need as much sleep."

Altair looked at the ladder to the roof tent, but he wasn't ready to sleep. "Can I stay down here with you for a bit?" he asked Magnús, who nodded.

They moved farther from the camper van, so they could talk without disturbing whatever it was Diwata and Ólafur were getting up to in there. It was past midnight, trees were sparse, and the night sky was clear.

Altair gazed up in wonder. "So many stars. In Boston, the sky never looks like this."

"Just wait," Magnús said. "A clear night like this, and it's likely you'll get to see—yes! Look over there."

Streaks of green had appeared in the sky, a ribbon of light with traces of purple, red, and blue.

"Oh. My. God." Altair was breathless. He'd always heard about the Northern Lights, had *hoped* he might see them on this trip, but...

"Oh my god," he repeated reverently.

As they watched, the ribbon thickened and changed. A curtain, emerald and violet, stretched above their heads, undulating, even more magical than anything Altair had seen in Hamarinn. The dancing lights shifted and multiplied across the night sky, like portals leading to another world.

"Are they?" he asked. "Portals to one of the other realms, I mean?"

"Not that I've ever heard. When I open the Hidden Ways through Álfheimur, the effect is different. But...who knows? Maybe there are hidden ways to other of the Nine Realms."

"The Rainbow Bridge to Asgard," Altair said, then grinned. "I know that one from the movies."

"You may be right." Magnús was looking at Altair, though,

not at the amazing display above their heads. A small smile graced his lips. "I have taken the aurora for granted since, well, for quite a while. Thank you for reminding me how special these things are."

He leaned down a bit, bringing his face closer. Altair's heart began thumping in his chest. Magnús stretched out his hand to brush across Altair's cheek. "Your skin is so warm," he said in a low tone. "I'd forgotten how much brighter the flames burn in a mortal body."

Altair gathered his courage and took a step closer to the elf. Trembling, he covered Magnús's fingers with his own. "Your hand is—"

That was all he had time for before a terrible shriek filled the air, and Magnús's ring of protective stones burst into a brilliant yellow light. The sound was so intense and painful, it drove Altair to his knees, hands held over his ears.

Magnús whirled, searching the landscape around them as he pulled a dagger from his belt. A blur of orange crashed into him from the side, sending the elf sprawling in the dirt. His blade flew from his hand.

Whatever had hit him disappeared as quickly as it had come. Altair stayed frozen on his knees. Between the noise, the light, and the unexpected attack, he had no idea what to do.

Diwata and Ólafur tumbled out of the camper van, their clothes in some disarray. Diwata made a gesture, and the horrible screeching noise ceased.

"What's happening?" she called out.

"Watch out!" Altair cried. "There's something fast—"

The orange blur rushed at Ólafur, and he went flying. His head slammed into the camper van with a sickening thud, and he crumpled to the ground.

"Óli!" Diwata screamed. She fumbled with her pouch, but before she could get anything out of it, the blur kicked her feet out from under, and Diwata's pouch flew out of her hands.

Altair stood alone in the center of the campsite. The brilliant glow from Magnús's stones made it as bright as day in a circle, but he couldn't see beyond the ring of light. Whatever was attacking them was using the darkness beyond the ring to hide.

Magnús groaned in the dirt and pushed one hand against the ground to try to rise.

"The lights. Can you turn off your light circle?" Altair hissed at him.

Magnús muttered a word and his wards dimmed, then vanished. The green glow of the Northern Lights illuminated the clearing just enough for Altair to see Magnús regain his feet and reach for his dagger. This time when the blur approached, Altair registered something running on four legs. It was covered with fur that, even tinted by the green glow of the aurora, seemed orange, and it had a long tail.

"It's the ghoul cat!" he yelled, even as Magnús hit the earth again. Altair heard the snap of a bone and Magnús's deep groan.

The creature stopped, standing over Magnús's prone body, tail lashing. She grinned widely at Altair, teeth as menacing in the sickly light as he remembered.

"This will reflect badly on your evaluation," the ghoul cat said in Ellen Sigmundsdóttir's voice. "You are supposed to be with me, far from here. What will the grant donors say?" She hissed a laugh.

"Don't hurt anyone. Please," Altair begged.

"I'm afraid that running after you has left me rather hungry. A quick snack of this broken toy, and then we'll be off. Hmm?"

The ghoul cat reached down and pulled Magnús to a standing position. He moaned and clutched the ribs on his left side with his hand. Without thinking, Altair hurled himself at the creature, wrapping one arm around her waist and, with the other hand, yanking on her tail. The cat dropped Magnús as she tumbled to the ground, Altair wrapped around her.

She hissed furiously at him and struggled. The ghoul cat was far stronger than Altair, but she seemed to be trying not to damage him. Perhaps she was under some kind of order? Altair held on tighter, hoping whatever instructions there were would keep him safe.

She stank of dirt and rot, nothing like a real cat. Claws scratched his back and his front as the cat forced her rear legs between them to push Altair away.

"Yrowr!"

The cat shrieked as something hard hit her on the head. Ólafur turned visible just a foot away, silver blood dripping down his grim face, a thick branch in his hands. He swung again, but the cat managed to shift around so the blow landed on Altair's back instead. He yelped and lost his grip. The cat tossed him aside and turned her attention to Ólafur.

The elf vanished, but the cat grinned. "I can smell your blood, álfur. Your tricks won't save you from me." She leapt, grappled something unseen, and brought it to the ground. Ólafur turned visible again, screaming from the teeth buried in his shoulder.

A glowing blue stone hit the cat in the eye. She dropped Ólafur and turned furiously on Magnús, who had braced himself against the picnic table and was launching his runestones. Altair could hear a painful wheeze in Magnús's voice as he drew breath for each spell, and he recalled Magnús saying his supply of stones was low.

A sudden gust of icy wind blew through the camp. The green light of the aurora dimmed and failed, because snow was suddenly falling, and the winds were growing in strength. Just enough light remained that Altair could see the effect was limited to their immediate area. Then he spotted Diwata on the ground, objects around her, a book in her lap and words falling from her lips that felt, even from a distance, thick and full of power.

The cat crouched close to the ground, buffeted by winds around her, calculating how to end this new annoyance. Before she could act, the snowstorm increased further, swirling flakes, shards of ice, and cyclonic winds taking it to a full blizzard in the campsite.

Altair shivered violently and tried to stagger in the direction he thought Magnús had stood. A blue glow flashed through the blizzard; the ghoul cat yowled. She was closer than Altair had expected. He thought he could hear words on the winds of the storm, but they sounded like the voices of Magnús and Ólafur. Something about retrieving a bag from the van, and Ólafur saying "I have it!"

Abruptly, the blizzard stopped. Everything in the campsite was covered with snow. The few trees were either blown over or bent under the weight of an ice coating their branches. The ghoul cat crouched close to the ground, her wet fur and tail drawing a menacing growl from her throat.

Magnús stood next to Ólafur, a gun in his hand. "Urðarköttur!" he yelled. "It's back to the grave with you." And he fired. Twice.

The explosion of noise was deafening. Altair could almost see streaks of silver flying from the gun at the cat. She leapt to escape, but the bullets caught her in mid-air. She shrieked and flailed, claws extended, kicking wildly as she fell straight at Altair. He had no chance to move, even to breathe, before sharp claws connected with his face, his chest and belly. The moment was so fast he didn't register anything more than shock before the still body of Ellen Sigmundsdóttir landed on top of him.

Magnús yelled, sounding horrified, and Altair could hear him running closer. But he couldn't see from one eye, and he was wet from chest to belly. He lay under the dead woman, aware of pain, aware of bleeding.

I'm dying, he thought. *I'm blind, and I'm bleeding to death.*

Magnús reached him and hurled the professor's body aside.

He dropped to his knees. Through one eye, Altair could see him looking, horror-struck, at the wounds all over Altair's body.

"I-I'm so sorry, Gods, Altair! I'm so sorry!"

Ólafur and Diwata limped up to stand behind Magnús, their mouths agape in disbelief.

"I should have been stronger," Diwata said, moaning. "With the blizzard. If I could have kept her trapped longer..."

"Altair," Ólafur said, his eyes wet. "Let me in your mind. I will hold you company there until...until..."

Altair felt Magnús lay hands gently on his bloody chest, and tears dripped down onto his face. The pain, surprisingly, wasn't getting worse. Magnús muttered words and called hoarsely on gods whose names Altair didn't know.

"It's all right," Altair managed to get out. It was hard to breathe, but he wanted Magnús to know. "You did everything you could."

A whisper of wind stirred his hair then. Was Diwata calling up another storm? No, she was still there, head on Ólafur's shoulder, sobbing. Ólafur didn't seem to notice the warm wind that had arisen either. None of them seemed to hear the pulsing in the ground, underneath Altair's back, or perhaps inside his chest like a second heartbeat.

Is this death?

The pulse was inside him, warm and kind. He could almost hear words, and he wondered if it was his mother. Maybe even the father who had abandoned him as a young boy. Maybe they had come to help him die peacefully. What was it whispering...?

"—While the eagle lives, the falcon lives. Use the blade to know thyself—"

That wasn't his mother's voice. Not even that of his father, though he'd last heard it decades before. This voice was full of strength and certainty. The pulse in his chest grew stronger.

"By the Allfather!" Magnús's eyes were open wide as he stared down at Altair's chest. There was a weird tickling sensation there. It reached his eyes, and Altair blinked in annoyance. It wasn't fair to die with odd feelings like that.

"Altair," Diwata breathed, amazement in her voice. "I can't believe what I'm seeing."

Altair looked up at her, only then realizing he could see out of both eyes. "What's happening?" he asked, lifting his head to look down at himself.

His shirt was shredded, his skin was covered in dried blood, but his skin... It was whole. Only some scratches remained, and they already looked like they were days old. He raised a hand to his face and felt more dried blood, but nothing hurt any longer.

Ólafur dropped to his knees, in a reverent posture. "This is a blessing from the Æsir, surely. Beyond any gift I've ever heard tell of."

Weariness suddenly overwhelmed Altair. He wanted to tell them about the voice he'd heard, the words... What were they? Something about a falcon and a blade...

No, they were gone. The only thing he remembered was that he was loved.

The dancing Northern Lights faded away. Altair's last sight was the face of Magnús, filled with anguish, determination, and... something more.

Then darkness took him.

EPILOGUE

In a vast cavern somewhere, water dripped into a well. Large boulders upon which runes were carved lined the walls. The roots of an enormous ash tree came right through the roof of the cavern. A serpent lay coiled among those roots, its tongue flicking occasionally to touch the wood.

Three bonfires cast flickering shadows on stone and upwards to dance in the roots of the tree. In those shadows were flickers of men and women, elves and gods. Some of the shadows looked to the past for guidance, others to the future for hope, and still others straight forward, into the present, for wisdom.

Three females—it would be disrespectful to call them women, or even goddesses, because they came before the gods—sat on wooden thrones arranged around a central loom. Needles clicked in their hands as they wove skeins of yarn into a tapestry that already folded over and over itself an infinite number of times.

Urður paused to loosen a single thread from her spindle. The thread was somehow white, blue, and silver at the same time. She stretched out her arms, draping the length of thread in her hands.

"A long life indeed, sisters, with many colors of joy and grief to enrich our work."

Verðandi reached forward to snatch the thread from Urður's hands. "It is not given to you to measure the length, sister." She drew the thread taut, her arms impossibly long. "Let me see. Four hundred years and more are gone already, and a little bit remains to be used in our tapestry."

Skuld leaned close to Verðandi, a pair of silver shears in her hand. She positioned the dangling end of thread between the blades of her shears, only to close them with a sharp snap. "As we planned, sisters. The Guardian's thread has been woven with the Falcon's. Magnús of the Hidden Ways has taken the first step to meet his doom."

EXCERPT FROM FALCONGUARD

The story of Magnús and Altair continues in FALCONGUARD, coming in April 2025. Here is the exciting first chapter...

Not thirty minutes after a ghoul cat had dealt a life-ending blow to Altair, Magnús stared after the miraculous human as Diwata took him to the nearby pond to clean off dried blood.

Altair had slept a bit after his inexplicable healing, Magnús keeping watch over him. When he woke, Ólafur pulled a shirt and pants from his pack for Altair to change into. Now the cousins tended to each other's wounds as best they could, watching Diwata and Altair walk away. Ólafur traced a glyph of healing in the air over Magnús's ribs, helping him to breathe easier.

Ólafur's mental voice carried amazement as he worked. «What in the name of Hela just happened?»

Magnús's mind rang with his own astonishment, and he could only shrug. He drew magic to power the glyph he sketched over

Ólafur. «I have no idea. Something that heals itself from life-ending wounds? I've never heard of such a creature.»

«Perhaps it's in the nature of Altair's magic, rather than his parentage. Diwata and I have been discussing ways to get at the enchantment that controls or threatens him. Maybe when we solve that, Altair's nature will reveal itself.»

Magnús walked over to the body of the dead woman who had been a ghoul cat. She was smallish as a human, less than half the size of the beast she became. Blood pooled in the gravel under her.

"What did you shoot her with?" Ólafur asked aloud.

"Silver bullets," Magnús said. "Bryndís told me that a mirror will mesmerize an urðarköttur for a time, though we don't know how Altair guessed that. Only silver bullets can kill it. Bryndís had someone pack the gun in with our supplies, but it didn't occur to me the beast would find us so easily."

He grunted in frustration. "I should have been better prepared. Altair would have died if he wasn't...whatever he is."

"And the prophecy says if Altair dies, Iceland dies." Ólafur was silent a moment. "You're too hard on yourself, cousin. You took every precaution, and when the attack came, we handled it. Altair was in the way, but that was bad luck, not a failing on your part."

Magnús just grunted. He knew he'd failed. As he always suspected he would. For the hundredth time, he wondered what the Nornir were doing, engaging him in this prophecy. Altair was more than a pawn of fate. He was a gentle, sparkling, young man who deserved a long and happy life. He needed someone stronger to keep him safe, someone with fewer failures on his balance sheet.

"You're thinking of Sigurjón, aren't you?" Ólafur asked. Magnús glared at him sharply, until Óli held up both hands placatingly. "I didn't look into your mind. But I know that brooding look, and it isn't hard to follow your thoughts from Altair to Sigurjón."

"Why do you say that?"

Ólafur cocked his head. "Surely you see it."

"Assume I don't."

"You were in love with a young human, and you felt like you failed him. Now you feel like you're failing Altair. Since you have feelings for him, it's natural you'd be reminded of the past."

"I'm not in love with Altair," Magnús responded immediately. He couldn't be. They'd just met. Yes, Altair was handsome. He had wit and courage, a spark of life that was precious, an air of self-effacement combined with backbone...

"I'm not," Magnús said again, more softly.

"Whatever you say, cousin." Ólafur lightly punched his shoulder. "It's been a century since you lost Sigurjón. There is no dishonor to his memory if you love another. Even in the best of circumstances, you will never have more than a mortal's lifespan to spend with any human. I can't believe someone worthy of your love would expect you to remain solitary after he dies."

"Anyway, Altair doesn't want to stay in Iceland. And don't forget the rest of that prophecy. What I may or may not want is irrelevant even if I succeed in whatever it is the Nornir expect of me."

"Your doom," Ólafur said gravely. "I know. But 'doom' is not the same thing as a death sentence."

Magnús could hear Altair and Diwata returning from the stream, talking softly. "No more, Óli. We can't talk about this around Altair without risking a seizure, and it doesn't matter anyway. Two days until the new moon. Less, really, since it's well after midnight. We need to sleep and get moving when it's light."

When the humans joined them, Diwata grimaced. "I can take care of that," she said, gesturing with her chin to the corpse. "After Lady Bryndís told us about the urðarköttur, I studied them a bit. They come from a cat buried in a graveyard, subjected to sorcery, and left for three years. I don't think they can rise a second time, but I've got a counter-spell that should help before we bury her."

"You two go rest," Ólafur said. "You need to be ready for Grýla. I'll keep watch the rest of the night with Diwata."

Magnús nodded wearily, then said, "That screaming noise. That was your spell, too?"

Diwata grinned. "It's from Óli's favorite metal band. I added it to your light stones in case we didn't see the flashing. Pretty great, wasn't it?"

Altair groaned. "It was so loud, I thought my ears would burst."

"Really?" Ólafur looked thoughtful. "The magic cry was intense but I wouldn't say painfully so. Did either of you experience pain with it?" Both Magnús and Diwata murmured denials. "Perhaps your race is one with exceptional hearing. Another clue we can work with."

"It was sharp, like it was cutting into my brain." Altair stopped talking suddenly, his eyes narrowing in concentration. "Cut. Something about a blade..."

"What about a blade?" Magnús asked.

"When *this* happened"—Altair gestured down as his chest and belly—"I think I heard a voice. It said something about finding a blade."

"May I?" Ólafur gestured vaguely at Altair's head. "Perhaps I can help find the memory."

"Um, I'd rather Magnús try. No offense, Óli. It's just...he's already been in there a lot."

Magnús tried to conceal the rush of pleasure in his belly. Altair trusted him still, even though Magnús's mistake about the urðarköttur should have killed him.

Although it wasn't necessary for mental contact, he rested his hand on Altair's shoulder and reached out gently with his huldufólk gifts. Altair's mind was so familiar to him already. Magnús skimmed the surface of it like a skater on a frozen pond, trying not to go too deeply though he selfishly wanted to know

Altair's private thoughts. He replayed recent memories—Altair and Diwata talking about magical energies and theories on how it worked, Altair shivering in the cold water as he cleaned blood from his body and wondered if Magnús would think he was too skinny—

Stop that, Altair said in his mind, chidingly. *Too personal.*

—Altair looking at the body of the person that was supposed to have been his mentor, Altair watching his wounds heal and hearing a voice in his head, the words so soft and vague he couldn't really remember, but yes, something about using the blade to know himself.

The memory was gone. Magnús disengaged their thoughts respectfully, but couldn't resist stroking Altair's hair before withdrawing his hand.

When he related the memory he'd found, Diwata chewed her lower lip thoughtfully. "A blade to help Altair know himself. It isn't reminding me of any spell I know, but I'll think about it."

"Perhaps Lady Bryndís will have some idea," Ólafur suggested.

The two wandered off, softly discussing how to proceed. Magnús leaned in and said quietly in Altair's ear, "You are not too skinny."

~

FALCONGUARD is coming April 4, 2025.

GLOSSARY

Terms, locations and gods appearing throughout FALCONSAGA:

Æsir: the principal pantheon of Norse gods

Akureyri: the second-largest city in Iceland, located to the north of the island

Álfaborg: the capital city of the huldufólk where Queen Hildur maintains her court; located beneath a hill in the human town of Borgarfjörður-Eystri

Álfar: the light elves from Álfheimur, also known in Iceland as the huldufólk

Álfheimur: one of the Nine Realms, the original home of the álfar or elves

Alþingi of Realms: a gathering of leaders from each of the Nine Realms to establish laws and adjudicate matters that affect more than one race of beings in Iceland, inspired by the first human parliament, called Alþingi

Ásgarður: one of the Nine Realms, the home of the Æsir

Askur and Embla: the first humans on Miðgarður, fashioned from an ash and an elm tree by the gods Óðinn, Vili and Vé

Bergrisi: one of the four Landvættir or land wights, in form a giant that guards the south of Iceland against sorcerous invasion

Black School, The: in legend, a school created by the Devil to train magicians

Borgarnes: a town north of Reykjavik, in a region where Egill Skallagrímsson, the poet-hero of Egil's Saga, had a farm

Brennivín: a clear, herbal, distilled liquor made in Iceland, usually from caraway or dill

Dökkálfar: the dark elves from Svartálfaheimur, who have power over shadows and are close kin to the álfar

Dreki: one of the four Landvættir or land wights, in form a dragon that guards the east of Iceland against sorcerous invasion

Dvergar: the dwarves from Niðavellir, who can move through solid stone

Egil's Saga: one of the great Icelandic family sagas, about the life of Egill Skallagrímsson

Egilsstaðir: a large town in the east of Iceland

Eyrbyggja Saga: one of the Icelandic sagas, about a long-standing feud between two chieftains

Fenrir: a monstrous wolf and son of Loki, who is foretold to kill Óðinn during Ragnarök

First Covenant: a law made at the original Alþingi of Realms, which states, "No being not of Iceland shall be told of or allowed to spread knowledge of Iceland's super-nature."

Forseti: the god of justice and reconciliation

Freyja: the goddess of magic, love, and fertility; one of the Vanir rather than the Æsir

Galdrabók: Icelandic for a spell book or grimoire

Galdur: a form of Icelandic magic using incantations

Gammur: one of the four Landvættir or land wights, in form a giant eagle that guards the north of Iceland against sorcerous invasion

Goði: a male chieftain; ; *see also* Gyðja

Griðungur: one of the four Landvættir or land wights, in form a giant bull that guards the west of Iceland against sorcerous invasion

Grýla the Trollmother: a troll reputed to make a soup from the bodies of naughty children, who are found and brought to her by the Yule Cat

Gyðja: a female chieftain; *see also* Goði

Hafnarfjörður: a town south of Reykjavik, known for its population of elves

Hákarl: fermented shark, a national dish of Iceland

Hallgrímskirkja: a Lutheran church in Reykjavik, the largest church in Iceland and one of its tallest buildings

Hamarinn: a city of the huldufólk, located beneath a park of the same name in the human town of Hafnarfjörður

Harpa: a concert hall in Reykjavik

Heimdallur: the god of foreknowledge who protects the realm of Ásgarður

Hel: the goddess of death and a daughter of Loki, who rules an area--also called Hel—that is located in the realm of Niflheimur

Hidden Ways: magical paths that connect Miðgarður to Álfheimur, and perhaps to other of the Nine Realms

Hólar: a town in the north of Iceland

Huldufólk: the term that the Álfar in Iceland use for themselves, signifying their ability to turn invisible at will

Jötunheimar: one of the Nine Realms, and home to the jötnar or frost giants

Keflavik: the international airport located near Reykjavik

Kjaftæði: Icelandic for "bullshit"

Landvættir: Icelandic for "land wights", the four mystical protectors of Iceland

Ljósálfar: the light elves who reside in Álfheimur rather than on Miðgarður

Loki: the god of mischief and sorcery

Manngjöld: a payment made in compensation for taking a life

Meili: the god of travel

Miðgarður: one of the Nine Realms, also known as Earth; home of humans, trolls, and certain wights or spirits

Mímir: the god of wisdom

Mountain King: title of the ruler of the trolls of Miðgarður

Muspellsheimur: one of the Nine Realms, home of the eldjötnar or fire giants; ruled by Surtur

Niðavellir: one of the Nine Realms, home of the dvergar or dwarves

Niflheimur: one of the Nine Realms, where some of the dead go; ruled by Hel

Nine Realms, The: the nine worlds connected by Yggdrasill

Nornir: three sister goddesses of destiny, who weave fate near the Well of Urd at one of the roots of Yggdrasill

Nykur: a water spirit, sometimes appearing as a horse

Óðinn: chief of the Norse pantheon, leader of the Æsir; also referred to as the Allfather

Pabbi: Icelandic term of endearment for a father

Plokkfiskur: an Icelandic dish of potatoes mashed with cod

Ragnarök: also called the Twilight of the Gods, the last battle between the Æsir and the forces of evil

Rauðskinna: a galdrabók reputed to contain many evil spells; also called the Red Book

Reykjanes: a peninsula south of Reykjavik with frequent volcanic activity

Reykjavik: the capital city of Iceland

Ring Road: a highway that circles the perimeter of Iceland

Sæmundur: an Icelandic bishop and hero of many folktales, sometimes referred to as the wisest human in Icelandic history

Seiður: a form of Icelandic magic using rituals

Skalla-Grímur Kveldúlfsson: the father of Egill Skallagrímsson, and possibly the son of a werewolf, who features prominently in Egil's Saga

Skuld: one of the Nornir, whose special province is the future

Skyr: an Icelandic form of yogurt

Sólfar: a famous sculpture located in Reykjavik

Spádómur: Icelandic for "prophecy"

Sundhöllin: one of many public swimming halls frequented by Icelanders of all ages

Sunstone: a piece of glass formed magically from a shard of glacial ice to hold light

Surtur: lord of the fire giants of Muspellsheimur

Svartálfaheimur: one of the Nine Realms and home to the dökkálfar

Þór: the god of thunder and battles, known for his hammer Mjölnir

Týr: the god of war and justice

Urðarköttur: a ghoul-cat, created by burying the corpse of a cat in a graveyard for three years; can be trapped in its own reflection but can only be killed by silver buttons or bullets

Urður: one of the Nornir, whose special province is the past

Valhöll: the hall in Ásgarður where honored warriors who die in battle reside until Ragnarök

Vanaheimur: one of the Nine Realms, home of the Vanir who warred with the Æsir and lost

Vanir: the secondary pantheon of Norse gods, including Freyja and her brother Freyr

Veðurfölnir: servant of Gammur

Verðandi: one of the Nornir, whose special province is the present

Vili and Vé: brothers of Óðinn

Yggdrasill: the World Tree, an immense ash tree and center of the cosmos that connects the Nine Realms

Ýmir: the first jötnar or frost giant, whose body was used by Óðinn and his brothers to form the cosmos

242

Acknowledgments

I hope you enjoyed the first part of the story of Magnús and Altair. If you liked FALCONSAGA, please consider leaving a review on Amazon, Goodreads, or any other social media. Ratings and reviews are incredibly helpful to independent authors like me.

Thank you to Erica Pike for helping me with Icelandic names and details. Please attribute any remaining errors with Icelandic names, idioms and locations to the mischievous huldufólk.

Thanks as well to Andrew Hodges and Sara Kelly for their editorial assistance, to Kangsoon Park for my new author photo, and to Colin Abbott for his beautiful cover.

About the Author

Robert Winter is an award-winning romance novelist and recovering lawyer. When he turned 50, Robert left behind the (allegedly) glamorous world of international law firms and bankruptcy court to pursue his real passion. Now he lives in Montreal and on Cape Cod with his husband, studying French between trips to exotic locations.

Contact Robert at the following links:
Website http://robertwinterauthor.com
Facebook robert.winter.921230
Goodreads 16068736.Robert_Winter
Bluesky rwinterauthor.bsky.social
Email RobertWinterAuthor@comcast.net

ALSO BY ROBERT WINTER

Pride and Joy series

September

Asylum

Nights at Mata Hari series

Every Breath You Take

Lying Eyes

Holidays Suck! series

Vampire Claus

Fangsgiving

(Part 3 coming in 2025)

And writing as M.J. Edwards

The Escort's Tale